Color Me Criminal

by Ellen Weiss & Mel Friedman
Illustrated by S. M. Taggart

*Based on the computer software
created by Brøderbund Software, Inc.*

HarperTrophy®
A Division of HarperCollinsPublishers

HarperTrophy is a registered trademark of
HarperCollins Publishers Inc.

Color Me Criminal

Library of Congress Cataloging-in-Publication Data
Weiss, Ellen 1949–
  Color me criminal / by Ellen Weiss and Mel Friedman ; illustrated by
S. M. Taggart
  "Based on the computer software created by Brøderbund Software, Inc."
    p.   cm.   (A Carmen Sandiego mystery)
  Summary: Young ACME detectives, eleven-year-old Ben and nine-year-old
Maya, are on the trail of the elusive thief Carmen Sandiego, suspected of
stealing the colors from the Painted Desert.
  ISBN 0-06-440663-6 (pbk.)
  [1. Painted Desert (Ariz.) 2. Mystery and detective stories.] I. Friedman,
Mel. II. Taggart, S. M., ill. III. Series.
PZ7.W4472Clo   1997   96-29073
[Fic]—dc20   CIP
                                                                    AC

Typography by Steve Scott
1 2 3 4 5 6 7 8 9 10
❖
First Edition

For Sam, who
knows everything

Prologue
Painted Desert, Arizona, USA

The shack was in the middle of the Arizona desert, with nobody around for miles. But that was how the old man liked it. He liked the broiling, dry heat in the daytime and the sudden chill at night. He liked the silence broken only by the sounds of small things scurrying into their burrows to escape the sun. And most of all, he liked the colors. For this was the Painted Desert. Here, Mother Nature had taken her paintbrush, loaded with iron oxide, and had created a dazzling landscape of oranges, reds, chocolates, lavenders, greens, and purples. The colors seemed to shift and change constantly. The old man liked nothing better

1

than to sit in the half-busted rocking chair in front of his shack and watch the show.

But this morning was different. This morning, very early, the old man had awakened to the sound of a howling windstorm that sounded as if a freight train were about to flatten his little shack. His tin roof shook until he thought it might get torn right off the house, pulling the nails with it. His shutters banged endlessly.

The man sat up in bed and pulled his boots on. He knew he'd better get outside and grab his rocking chair before it blew clear to Flagstaff.

He leaned his shoulder against the door, using all his strength against the wind. Finally the door gave, and he was able to wriggle outside. The door slammed shut behind him.

The rocking chair was long gone. The windstorm was blinding, whipping the sand so hard that it stung his skin and hurt his eyes. He shaded his eyes now with both hands, trying to see. Something didn't look right. What was it?

He stepped away from his shack, leaning into the wind, his sparse white hair whipping around his head. Then he rubbed his eyes and looked again.

Something was dreadfully wrong with the Painted Desert. The colors were all gone, as if someone had sucked them right out of the landscape. It looked just like a black-and-white movie.

1

ACME Headquarters, San Francisco, California

"**I**s there any more of that caramel popcorn?" Maya asked Ben.

"No, we finished it two hours ago," Ben replied. "All we have left are those disgusting cheese-ball things." He didn't look up from the ACME computer, which he was checking for a virus.

Maya suddenly jumped up from the sofa. "I'm so *bored*!" she yelled. "Bored, bored, bored!" She leaped back onto the sofa and started jumping up and down on it, yelling "Bored!" with every bounce.

"I don't think your aunt would like it too much if she saw you doing that," said Ben mildly.

"So what?" said Maya. "What if she is The Chief? That doesn't give her the right to stick me—I mean us—with office duty while everybody else is away on an adventure!"

"Actually, it does. Besides, somebody has to hold down the fort while they're gone."

"She's just punishing us for screwing up last time, and you know it, Ben."

Ben did know it. Just a month ago Ben and Maya had had their first royal foul-up as ACME detectives. It was that fateful day Carmen Sandiego had tried stealing the Golden Gate Bridge. They'd had her in their grasp, but she'd slipped away at the last minute. Though the bridge was back in San Francisco where it was supposed to be, Carmen had disappeared into the fog, ready to steal again. Since then Ben and Maya had been in the doghouse, demoted to lowly gumshoes. "I don't know what I was thinking, letting you do real detective work," The Chief had said, shaking her head. "You're just kids. You'll have to get a little older before I try that again."

It was true that Ben was eleven and Maya was only nine, but they weren't just any kids. They were special. They were smart. They were tough. They were brave. And Maya, of course, being The

Chief's niece, had detective work in her genes. The kids just knew they could do better next time.

But for the time being, they were stuck minding the store at ACME headquarters. Every single ACME detective, along with The Chief, had rushed halfway across the Pacific Ocean to protect the international date line. A report had come in yesterday that Carmen and her henchpeople were planning to steal it.

"Sorry to be dumb," Ben had said to Maya, "but what exactly *is* the international date line? I don't know as much about geography as you do."

"Understatement of the year," said Maya, rolling her eyes. "Okay, I'll explain it. It's not exactly a line, not that you can see, anyhow. But you know how when it's six o'clock in New York, it's three o'clock in San Francisco?"

"Sure," said Ben.

"Well, the international date line is where it's, like, zero o'clock. It's the place where one day ends and the next day starts. So east of the line it's Thursday, and west of the line it's Friday."

"So, if Carmen stole the date line, it would never get to be tomorrow?"

"Bingo," Maya had said.

And that was why The Chief and every single ACME operative she could get her hands on were camped out all along the international date line, from the North Pole to the South Pole.

The red ACME phone rang, and Maya stopped bouncing. She and Ben looked at each other. That phone rang only when there was an emergency.

Maya made a dive for it. "Hello?" she panted.

The cracked voice on the other end of the phone was so excited, she could barely make out what it was saying. It sounded like an old man.

"Excuse me?" she said. "A fainted buzzard?"

Ben heard the little voice in the phone buzzing madly.

"Ohhh," said Maya. "The Painted Desert—in Arizona. What's the problem there?"

She listened some more.

"The colors? They've been stolen?"

Ben turned away from his work on the computer and listened harder to the conversation. The colors stolen from the Painted Desert? This could be the work of only one person.

Hmmm, looks like this is turning into my most colorful caper yet. They don't call me the Queen of Crime for nothing. So far, everything is working exactly as I'd planned it—of course. But this is just the beginning. Before I'm done, things are going to look very different for ACME and those two young detectives. Very different indeed.

2
ACME Headquarters, San Francisco, California

"**H**oly cow!" said Maya, hanging up the phone. "The colors have been stolen from the Painted Desert! What'll we do?"

"Everybody's gone," said Ben.

"That means it's up to us," said Maya, her jaw set. "We'd better get on the case!"

"Whoa," said Ben. "Maybe we shouldn't move quite so fast. Let's check in with The Chief first. She'll know what we should do."

"We aren't supposed to bother her unless it's really important."

"If this isn't important, what is?" Ben said.

"Okay," agreed Maya. "Let's get her on the Sender."

The Ultra-Secret Sender was the very latest ACME gadget. In addition to being a phone and camcorder, it also had a fax, translator, decoder, and access link to the Internet and the ACME CrimeNet database. All this in a little box the size of a personal tape player. On one side of the box was a panel that could flip down to become a phone mouthpiece, revealing a tiny video screen. On the other side were a miniature computer screen and keyboard.

Maya sat down with the Sender and punched in the secret code that she knew would connect her directly to The Chief. She waited, listening to the beeps and blips while her call went through. It seemed to Maya that there were more beeps and blips than usual; must be because The Chief was somewhere in the Pacific, east of Wake Island.

"Hello!" came a familiar voice finally. The connection was bad, and The Chief sounded crabby.

"Hi, Chief. It's Maya." Maya never called The Chief "Aunt Velma." In fact, almost nobody in the world knew The Chief's real name was Velma.

"Oh, Maya. Hiya, kid. What's up?"

"Well, we have a little problem here."

"It'd better be more than a leaking faucet. I'm superbusy here, trying to stake out an imaginary line that's thousands of miles long. The weather's been lousy, the sea is rough, there's no sign of Carmen or anyone from V.I.L.E., and if you must know, I'm feeling pretty darned seasick!"

"I'm sorry to bother you, Chief," said Maya. "And you know I wouldn't call if it wasn't really, really important. But it looks like somebody's stolen all the colors from the Painted Desert."

"Nothing's come through to me on the Crime-Net. Where did you get this information?"

"It was phoned in on the red phone. The informant said he's an ACME stringer. Name's Loco Moshun. Old guy."

The Chief snorted. "Maybe he doesn't know it," she said, "but Loco Moshun is an *ex*-ACME stringer. He's called in sightings of flying saucers and Elvis once too often. Little problem with the cactus juice, if you ask me. He's a totally useless informant. You'd better check your sources, and don't bother me with nonsense next time. And Maya?"

"Yes, Chief?"

12

"Stop eating those cheese-ball things. I want you and Ben to eat some vegetables, okay?"

"Right, Chief."

After she hung up, Maya collapsed onto the sofa in a depressed heap.

"What'd she say?" Ben asked her.

"She said we screwed up again." Maya sighed. She repeated what The Chief had said about Loco.

"I guess we're really in the doghouse now," said Ben. He turned off the computer. "Maybe we *are* too young to be ACME detectives."

"Don't be silly," said Maya. "We're just as good detectives as anybody else. We'll show them."

"I don't know," said Ben. "Maybe we should just forget it."

Maya snapped her fingers. "You know what?" she said. "There's an easy way to see whether Loco hallucinated the whole thing or not."

"What's that?"

"We can look at the satellite photos."

"Right!"

ACME had its own spy satellite, and it was so powerful that it could read the ingredients on a candy bar wrapper from five hundred miles up. If the colors really were missing from the Painted

Desert, the satellite would definitely pick it up.

Maya tapped her code word into the Ultra-Secret Sender to access the CrimeNet. "Now all we have to do is wait," she said, putting the Sender down on the sofa beside her.

Sure enough, a couple of minutes later the Sender began beeping. Maya picked it up and looked at the message on its screen.

"That's our satellite photo," she said. She punched some numbers into the Sender. Then she punched in some more, looking more and more frustrated. Finally she banged it down onto the desk. "I can't get the stupid satellite picture," she said to Ben. "I keep coming up with The Chief's recipe for oatmeal cookies."

Ben laughed.

"You'll have to do it," said Maya. "I hate it that you know how to do the computer stuff and I don't."

"Well, look at all the things you can do that I can't," said Ben. He picked up the gadget and casually punched a few keys.

"Like what?" she demanded.

"Like being strong. And being brave. And knowing everything about geography."

Maya considered these. "I guess you're right," she said.

"And being modest," added Ben.

Maya threw the last cheese ball at him.

"Okay, here it is," said Ben. "Now, let me just zoom in on the Southwest. . . . There it is. Where's the Painted Desert?"

"Northern Arizona," said Maya.

Ben pushed a couple of buttons, and then he gasped. "Look at this!" he said, handing Maya the Sender.

Maya could see the Grand Canyon, the Petrified Forest, the Hopi Indian Reservation—all the areas around the Painted Desert. They were all in color. But the Painted Desert was in black and white.

"It's true!" she crowed. "Loco was right!"

"What'll we do now?"

"We have to go there. You know as well as I do who's probably behind this. There's not a moment to lose. Are we going to let her get away again?"

"Not on your life!" said Ben.

Maya immediately dialed up Yul B. Gowen, ACME travel guy extraordinaire. When ACME agents had to go somewhere, Yul figured out how to get them there.

"Hmmm," said Yul after Maya had explained the problem. "I can't figure out how to get you there."

"You have to be kidding," she said.

"I never kid, kid," he said. "See, the problem is that all means of transport are already in use. I had to get every agent on earth to the international date line. Except you, that is."

"Don't rub it in."

"Hang on," he said. "I'm getting an idea." She heard him tapping keys in the background. "Okay, this'll work. I have a supersonic mail plane. Very fast. It goes right over Flagstaff, which is the nearest city."

"What do you mean, goes right over? It doesn't stop there?"

"Well, no. But not to worry. I'll outfit you with parachute hang gliders. They're foolproof. You'll jump right out over the Painted Desert, and there you'll be."

Maya snickered. "Wait till I tell Ben about this," she said. "This is right up his alley."

16

3
Painted Desert, Arizona

Twelve hours later, Ben and Maya were floating down gently over the Painted Desert, their backpacks secured and full of essential spy gear—toothbrushes and pajamas.

"I hate this!" Ben said through gritted teeth.

"Oh, lighten up," laughed Maya. "You just don't know how to have fun."

"Oh, sure," he replied, wrestling with the controls on his hang glider. "I bet crashing in the desert will be lots of fun."

"We won't crash. Besides, look at the view down there. When are you ever going to see something this amazing again in your life?"

He had to admit, it was pretty unbelievable. Off in the distance, the Echo Cliffs shimmered orange and pink in the heat. Directly below were the wind-carved rock formations of the Painted Desert. Black and white. Just like an old photo.

"The Painted Desert is supposed to have all kinds of colors," said Maya. "Red. Pink. Purple. Chocolate. Green. Lavender. Gray. I've read about it. It's supposed to be one of the most beautiful places on the planet. What's going to happen if it stays black and white? I can't even imagine what that would mean."

"Gosh," wondered Ben aloud, "I wonder what'll happen if I get squished when I land. Will I be a red mess, or black and white?"

"Shut *up*!" squealed Maya.

It really was time to land. Maya, who had tried hang gliding before, shouted directions to Ben, and they steered toward a flat-topped mesa. "Okay!" yelled Maya as the ground came rushing up toward them. "Don't forget to bend your legs!"

"Don't forget to what?" he said. But it was too late. He had already landed on his behind. "Ooh, that smarts," he said, standing up and dusting himself off.

"That was a beautiful landing," said Maya. "See? You could do it just fine."

"I don't know if I'm cut out to be an ACME agent," he grumbled.

Maya ignored him. "Now," she said, "if we can just figure out where Loco's shack is . . ."

"That's easy." Ben took the Ultra-Secret Sender out of his windbreaker. He punched in some coordinates, then squinted into the distance. "It should be . . . that way," he said, pointing west.

They started trudging in the direction of Loco's shack. Even though the desert was a desolate black and white, Ben and Maya were still in color. Actually, Ben's color was already beet-red from the scorching Arizona sun. Maya suddenly wished for some sunscreen. And a hat. And a pair of shades. She missed Headquarters already.

"It's a good thing you put the office on remote," said Maya.

"It should work," said Ben. "If we're lucky. Anything that comes into the office will be rerouted to us on the Sender."

They kept walking. It was throat-parchingly dry.

"How can anyplace be *this* hot in February?" Ben complained.

"The Southwest is always hot," Maya explained. "We should be thankful that Carmen didn't plan this caper for July. I guess we didn't remember to bring any water."

"What do you mean, 'we'?" Ben replied. "Maybe *you* didn't." He pulled a plastic water bottle out of his bag.

"Wow!" said Maya. "You brought us water!"

"What do you mean, 'us'?"

"Oh, pleeease, just give me a little."

"What'll you give me?"

"I'll give you a big punch in the nose if you *don't* share it," she declared.

Ben passed the bottle over. He could never say no to Maya anyhow, and she knew it. She was the natural leader of their little two-person pack. Besides being incredibly strong, she was also kinda cute. So she usually got her way.

Maya took a politely small sip of water and handed the bottle back. "That must be Loco's house over there," she said, pointing to a falling-down shack near the horizon.

"This place is so beautiful," said Ben. "It must look incredible in color."

"It used to be the bottom of a huge lake, you

21

know," Maya said. "Back in the Triassic Period. They've even found the fossils of small dinosaurs here."

As they walked along, Ben tried to imagine this baking desert at the bottom of a lake. It was pretty hard to do.

When they got close to the shack, they saw Loco immediately. He was up on the roof, nailing on shingles that had been torn off by the storm. He caught sight of them and waved.

"You the ACME agents?" he asked.

"Yup," said Maya.

"Pretty young for hotshot detectives, aren't you?" he called down, shading his eyes with his hand.

"We're old beyond our years," said Ben.

Loco climbed down from the roof. His face was tanned and weather-beaten, which made his pale blue eyes all the more striking.

"Don't you get lonesome out here all by yourself?" Maya asked him.

"Nope. I like it this way. Had enough of people a long time ago. I'm happier in the company of lizards."

"Could we ask you a few questions about what happened yesterday morning?" said Ben, pulling

22

out his little spiral notebook in a businesslike way.

"Ask away," said Loco. "I guess those big honchos at Headquarters thought I was crazy, huh? Well, I don't look so crazy anymore, do I?"

"No, sir," said Ben. "Now, when was the last time you saw the colors in the desert?"

"It was before the sun went down, night before last. After that, I wouldn't have been able to see whether the colors were there or not."

"And when did you discover that they were gone?"

"Musta been around six A.M. yesterday."

"Did you hear or see anything unusual during the night?" Maya asked him.

Loco stroked his chin. "Naw," he said. "Well, wait a second, there was a little something."

Ben and Maya pricked up their ears.

"What was it?"

"Along about two A.M., somebody came by here, right down this road. Sounded like a pickup truck, and it was in an awful big durned hurry."

"Is this the only road in or out of here?" Ben asked.

"Yup, it is. Come to think of it, though, I never heard the truck go back the other way."

"What's up this road?" asked Maya.

"Not much. Just a little lean-to up on Dagger Drop Mesa. But nobody's used it for years."

"Think we could have a look?" Ben asked.

"Sure," said Loco. "Hop in my jeep."

Loco's jeep looked like it was left over from World War II, but it ran fine. It took about half an hour of bumpy driving to get to Dagger Drop Mesa.

"There's the lean-to," Loco shouted over the noise of the motor.

The lean-to was leaning so far, it was just about touching the ground.

"Can we really go in there?" Ben asked.

"That thing's been standing for at least forty years," said Loco with a chuckle. "It'll probably stay up another ten minutes."

Carefully Ben and Maya pushed aside the tin door, which was hanging from one hinge. It was dark inside the shack, and there wasn't much in there: an old stained mattress on the floor, a beat-up table and chair, a tin plate and cup.

Maya walked over to the table. "What's this?" she said. She picked up a small white pad. It wasn't yellow and old, as everything else in the shack was; it looked new. A logo on top of each page announced: BIG MESA MOTEL. FREE CABLE IN EVERY ROOM.

"Hmmm," said Ben.

Maya took a closer look at it. "Rats," she said. "If somebody wrote on the last page, there's no evidence of it. No indentations, no nothing. I was hoping we could use the old rub-it-with-a-pencil trick."

Ben was fiddling with the Sender. After some difficulty, he pulled a small round lens from the bottom.

"What's that?" Maya asked him.

"Handy-dandy little gadget they just worked out," he said. "It's an ultraviolet scanner. It can see things the human eye can't make out."

"Holy cow," said Loco. "In my day, we used a magnifying glass."

Ben moved the lens up close to the pad and began to move it back and forth across the page. "Here goes nothing," he said. "There probably isn't anything on the pad."

But he was wrong. As they stared at the scanner's beam moving on the page, they began to be able to make out, very faintly, what looked like handwriting. It was glowing a strange shade of purple.

"Yes!" yelled Ben.

"Yippee!" Maya exulted. "We can read it!"

"Now we just have to figure out what it means," said Ben, peering at the words. He wrote down whatever they could make out on another sheet of the pad.

WHERE: THE BIG EASY, he wrote.

"Is that right?" he said. "That's not the name of a place."

"I think that's what it says," said Maya. "What's the next line?"

Ben squinted some more, and then wrote RENDEZVOUS: FAT TUESDAY.

"Stranger and stranger," said Maya.

"The last line's a real doozy," said Ben. He wrote it out: LOOK FOR: SAME CIGAR, NO END.

"Huh?" said Maya.

Loco had come over to huddle over the paper with them. He stroked his chin. "I think I can help you with the first line," he said.

"Great!" Maya said. "What the heck, or where the heck, is the Big Easy?"

"Well," he said, "I spent some time as a news-

paperman in the South—this was a while ago—
and down there, the Big Easy was what people
called New Orleans."

"Terrific name," said Maya. "The Big Easy.
Okay, so we know what that is. Now, what are we
going to do with the second line?"

"I have a little idea," said Ben. "I think *rendezvous* is a French word. I don't know what it
means, though."

"But it kind of makes sense," Maya said. "I
know that a lot of people in New Orleans speak
French. Ben, why don't you use the translator on
the Sender and see what it means?"

"Right," said Ben, punching it in. "It means
'meet,' " he answered.

"Okay, great. Now we have 'Meet: Fat
Tuesday.'"

"Hmmm," said Maya. "I'm stumped." She
paced the floor.

"Here's an idea," said Ben. "If we could trans-
late *rendezvous* from French to English, maybe we
could try translating *Fat Tuesday* from English to
French."

"But, *duh*, Ben," said Maya. "Then we'll have
some words in French. We don't speak French."

"Lemme just try it," Ben persisted.

The three of them stood over the Sender as Ben typed the words in. A second later, they all gave a great whoop together.

"*Mardi Gras!*" they yelled.

"We do speak a little French!" said Maya.

Ben punched in the code for the Sender's handy almanac and asked it when Mardi Gras would take place.

"Well, it's already late February, so let's see . . . holy cow!" he said. "It's tomorrow. We gotta go!"

"Maybe first we should see if we can make any sense out of the last line," suggested Loco.

"Right. 'Same cigar, no end.' What the heck does that mean?" said Maya.

"I don't see any cigar butts that have been left around here," said Ben.

"Maybe it's French too," said Maya. "Let's try translating it."

Ben punched it in. "*MÊME CIGARE, PAS FIN*" was the translation. They all scratched their heads.

"I don't think that worked," said Maya. "What else could it be?"

Ben, meanwhile, was writing some things on the pad.

"What are you doing?" Maya asked him.

"Just a silly hunch," he replied. "Sometimes when words look crazy, they're anagrams. You know—words with the letters all scrambled up."

Maya and Loco looked over Ben's shoulder as he tried to make different words with the letters in SAME CIGAR, NO END.

SAME RACE, NO DING

"Hmmm," said Maya.

SAME NICE DRAGON

"Nice dragon," she said. "Maybe there'll be a dragon float at Mardi Gras. We'll have to check."

A RINGED MESA CON

"Loco," said Ben, "is there a mesa around here called Ringed Mesa?"

"Nope," said Loco.

Ben kept shuffling letters around. Suddenly he gave out a little yelp. And then he wrote:

CARMEN SANDIEGO

4
Painted Desert, Arizona

Maya looked at Ben, and Ben looked at Maya. Loco looked at both of them.

"I guess that settles it," said Maya. "We're going to New Orleans."

"We'd better contact Yul and see if he can get us out of here."

They all piled into Loco's jeep again and headed back to his place. On the way, Ben dialed up the ACME travel department, and Yul appeared on the video screen, his bald head shining.

"Yul B. Gowen here."

"Yul," said Ben, "we've got a problem. We've got to get to New Orleans, pronto. Can you help us?"

"Anything for you, my little parsnips," said Yul. "Unfortunately, we've still got the same problem. Everything's taken." He scrunched up his face, thinking. "But I have an idea," he said. "Just stay where you are. In about half an hour, look out the window. We're going to fix you right up."

"Thanks a lot, Yul," said Ben. "I knew we could count on you."

Ben folded up the mouthpiece, but a second later there was an insistent beeping from the Sender. He folded it back down again, and there was Yul's tiny face, smiling out from the video screen again.

"Thought you were rid of me, didn't you?" chuckled Yul.

"Never!" said Ben.

"So, here's the thing," said Yul. "I just remembered something I was going to tell you."

"Okay, shoot," said Ben.

"Never say that!"

"Oops," said Ben. "Forgot I was talking to a member of the law-enforcement community."

"Right. Now," continued Yul, "here's the thing. Being as you're in the Southwest, and being as you're the only agents there—at least for the present time—

I thought I should alert you to something I noticed this morning while scanning my travel data banks— trains, planes, car rentals, all that stuff. There's been a lot of V.I.L.E. traffic to the Arizona area in the last couple of days."

"Oh, yes?" said Ben, his ears pricking up.

"Yessiree bob. Six V.I.L.E. operatives, in fact. Want to know who they are?"

"Definitely!" said Ben, scrambling to flip open the tiny computer on the other side of the Sender. "Okay, shoot."

"Never say that!"

"Oops, sorry."

"Here they are: Hugo Yurway. Liza Lotsa. Freda D. Darke. Dee Molish. Armand Geddon. And last but not least, Nell N. Void."

Ben typed madly to keep up. "Okay, got it," he said. "Thanks a lot, Yul!"

"We aim to please."

They said good-bye and hung up.

"Wow!" said Maya. "Six V.I.L.E. henchpeople! Something's up, for sure."

"I haven't had this much excitement since Elvis dropped in last May!" said Loco.

"Maybe they're all involved in this color-stealing

thing together—the henchpeople, I mean, not Elvis," said Ben.

"Or . . ." said Maya thoughtfully, "or maybe Carmen sent them all here to confuse us, so we wouldn't know who we're looking for."

"That would be just like her," said Ben. "But we're just a little too smart for her, aren't we?"

They exchanged a high five.

Meanwhile, Loco was looking out the window. "Well, wouldja look at that?" he said in amazement.

Maya and Ben looked. Outside the shack were two sleepy-eyed little burros. On their woolen saddle blankets were woven the letters *ACME*.

"Yul sent us burros!" said Ben.

"They're so cute!" said Maya.

"Cute but stubborn," said Loco. "If you can get them to go, you'll be lucky."

The Sender beeped once again. Maya answered. It was Yul.

"Here's how you get them to go," Yul said. "In their saddlebags you'll find sticks. Tied to the ends of the sticks are carrots on long strings. You get on the burros, hold the sticks up, and dangle the carrots in front of them. They'll go. When you get to the airport, you can give the burros the carrots."

"Then what do we do with them?" asked Maya.

"I've taken care of all the details. Just ask Loco to point you toward the airport. There are compasses in the saddlebags too. Maintain a steady west-by-southwest heading, and you'll be there in no time."

Four hours later Ben and Maya were standing at the entrance to the little Flagstaff airport. The sun burned hotly. Maya was feeding the burros carrots and water from a paper cup, and Ben was complaining about his extremely sore behind. "I'm going to get Yul for this," he grumbled.

An overweight man in a cowboy hat and large dark glasses walked up to them from across the parking lot. He flashed an ACME badge, gathered up the reins of the burros, and walked off, singing, "You ain't nothing but a hound dog."

"Hey," Maya said as the stranger walked away. "Didn't that guy look a lot like . . ."

"Elvis!" both kids said at once. But by then, the mysterious stranger had disappeared.

Inside the airport, they found tickets waiting for them. The plane would be leaving in just ten minutes.

"Boy, Yul really has faith in us, doesn't he?" said Maya. "He knew we'd get here on time."

"The seats on that plane better be soft, that's all I can say," said Ben.

In a little while they had settled into their extremely comfortable seats on the plane. The flight attendant had given them each several bags of peanuts, and they munched away as they watched the beautiful landscape below them get smaller and smaller.

"I don't care if Loco does see flying Elvises and aliens," said Ben. "I like him."

"Me too," said Maya.

The Sender beeped. "What does Yul want now?" Ben wondered aloud. He flipped the receiver down, and the man in the seat in front of them craned his neck to see what on earth that noise had been.

When the image came in on the video screen, Ben and Maya went rigid. It was The Chief!

"Uh, hi, Chief," said Ben.

"Just checking in," said The Chief. "How are things at Headquarters?"

"Great," said Ben weakly. "Just great. Everything's quiet."

"That's because all the action's here," said The

35

Chief. "All right, don't get too bored. I'll check in again tomorrow."

Ben hung up, letting out a shaky breath. "Whew!" he said. His forehead had broken out in a cold sweat.

"If we're wrong," said Maya, "we're in big trouble."

"*Big* trouble," agreed Ben.

"But we're not wrong," said Maya. "I know it."

"We'd just better not mess this up," said Ben.

"I'll tell you what," said Maya. "Let's use the CrimeNet to pull up the dossiers for the six V.I.L.E. agents Yul told us about. Then we can start figuring out who we're looking for."

"Good idea," said Ben.

Maya took the Sender from Ben and punched in the information she wanted. In a minute, the dossiers of all six V.I.L.E. operatives flashed on the screen, one by one.

The two kids stared at the dossiers for a few minutes.

"Okay," said Maya at last. "What do they tell us?"

"Not much," grumbled Ben. "We don't have anything to go on yet."

FREDA D. DARKE: BLACK HAIR, GREEN EYES.
HIGHLY PARANOID. HOBBY: PAINTING. FOOD: ITALIAN.

ARMAND GEDDON: BLACK HAIR, GRAY EYES.
LIKES JAZZ. HOBBY: GARDENING. FOOD: FRENCH.

LIZA LOTSA: BLACK HAIR, BROWN EYES.
COMPULSIVE LIAR. LOVES EMERALDS.
HOBBY: STARGAZING. FOOD: FRENCH.

DEE MOLISH: BLOND HAIR, GRAY EYES. BAD TEMPER.
HOBBY: PAINT-BY-NUMBER CLOWN PORTRAITS.
FOOD: FRENCH.

NELL N. VOID: BLOND HAIR, BLUE EYES.
LAWYER. HOBBY: CARD GAMES.
FOOD: FRENCH.

HUGO YURWAY: BROWN HAIR, BROWN EYES.
FORMER BODYBUILDER. HOBBY: PAINTING.
FOOD: VEGETARIAN.

Dee Molish

Nell N. Void

Armand Geddon

Freda D. Darke

Hugo Yurway

Liza Lotsa

"I have one idea," said Maya. "We could prob-ably eliminate Freda D. Darke."

"How come?"

"Because we know that the crime was definitely committed at night. When Loco went to bed, the colors were there. When he got up, they were gone."

"And?"

"And Freda's scared to death of the dark."

"Good thinking!" said Ben.

"Maybe we can't eliminate her for sure," said Maya. "Maybe she was scared but she did it anyway."

Ben groaned. "Maybe," he agreed.

They spent another hour going over and over the dossiers, but couldn't get any further. In two more hours they were in New Orleans.

Sometimes I really amuse myself. It's kind of fun being a devil in a red coat, stirring up trouble. The trail we laid in the desert was perfect, and now those rookies are off to New Orleans. I must say, I like being ahead of this game, pulling the strings from behind the scenes. First I send almost everybody at ACME on a wild-goose chase to the international date line. Then I give those detectives-in-training a little challenge of their own.

I can't wait to see what happens next.

5
New Orleans, Louisiana

New Orleans was a zoo. The airport was jammed with people, almost all of them hopped up and ready to party. They were headed for the biggest party in the South: Carnival.

"What is Mardi Gras, anyhow?" Ben asked Maya. He was trying to hold on to his backpack, which threatened to be swept away by the crush of people.

"I happen to have picked this up at the information desk," said Maya smugly, waving a small pamphlet. She opened it up and started scanning it. "It's a Catholic tradition," she explained. "New Orleans has a long history as a Catholic city, under both the French and the Spanish. Mardi Gras, or Fat Tuesday, is the day before Ash Wednesday, which is the first day of Lent. During Lent people give up a lot of things, like favorite foods, until Easter. So Carnival is people's last chance to eat, drink, and be merry before they have to get serious. The party starts in January and builds up until . . . today!"

"I guess that's why they call it Fat Tuesday."

"Guess so."

They hopped a bus into the city, jammed in among the crowd of hot, happy visitors. When they got off, they walked a block and found themselves on a street teeming with dancing revelers. Floats drifted down the street, and people in outrageous costumes were throwing beads and fake gold coins down to the crowds, who scrambled to catch them. Above the rooftops, evening was falling.

A thousand aromas of food cooking wafted into their noses, and Ben and Maya suddenly realized that they were very hungry.

"What are those wonderful-looking things?" Ben asked as they passed a booth. Inside, a man was making little puffs of fried dough and then sprinkling them with powdered sugar.

43

"Beignets, my boy!" said the man heartily. "Best treat on earth. Here, I'll let you try one free, just because I like you."

Ben bit into it, and a huge smile lit up his face. "This *is* the best treat on earth!" he said.

"Here's one for your friend," said the man, handing one to Maya.

"Now I know why they call this city the Big Easy," said Maya, chewing happily on her beignet. "People are *nice* here."

"Nobody's in a big hurry, like they are up in Noo Yawk," laughed the man, making fun of a New York accent. "Everybody takes time to enjoy life down here."

"Well, thanks for the beignets," said Ben. "They're great."

"Ben, look!" Maya yelped, grabbing his sleeve and pointing down the street.

Ben strained to see what she was pointing at, and then he spotted it. Disappearing around a corner was a dramatic figure in a red trenchcoat and red fedora, with billowing dark hair.

"Carmen!" cried Ben.

The kids took off after the figure. It wasn't easy to give chase, though, with thousands of costumed

people jamming the street. They lurched their way through the crowd, trying to spot the figure again.

"There she is!" said Maya. And there indeed was the red-clad figure, half a block ahead of them.

"Wait a second," said Ben. "There she is!" He pointed directly across the street, where a flash of red was moving in the opposite direction.

"This is crazy," said Maya, pointing up at a rooftop nearby, "but *there* she is!" The scarlet-coated figure was silhouetted for a second against the evening sky, and then disappeared.

Ben and Maya stopped running. "What's going on here?" Ben said.

"You know what I think?" said Maya. "I think there are a lot of imposters here, just to confuse us. The real Carmen Sandiego probably isn't here at all."

"Hey!" shouted Ben, lunging for yet another Carmen who was just vanishing down an alley right beside them. "Wait!"

The figure, of course, did not wait. In a moment it was gone, like a puff of smoke.

The French Quarter of New Orleans has many houses that are decorated with wrought iron, and the house in front of Ben and Maya was no exception. Maya bent down and closely examined the black curlicues of metal.

"*Aha!*" she crowed, standing up. "Look what we have here."

She extended her hand to Ben, and in it was a small clump of red threads. "Must have ripped off the outfit when that last Carmen was getting away," she said.

"These threads could be a gold mine for us," said Ben. "Maybe we can learn something by analyzing them."

"How are we going to do that?"

"New feature on the Sender," Ben said. "Very high-tech." He pushed a small button on the back of the Sender as Maya watched in fascination. Out popped a small plastic tube. "You just stick the thing you need analyzed in here," he explained, "like so." He carefully poked the thread down into the tube and pushed a button that made the tube retract into the Sender. "Then you just press this button here—the one that says ANALYZE."

He pushed that button, and the Sender began making little squeaky and chirpy noises. "The Sender can do a basic molecular analysis of the stuff," Ben told Maya, "and then it sends the information back via satellite to the ACME CrimeLab, where they interpret the information. They should be calling us any minute."

They had just seen two more Carmens when the phone beeped. Ben flipped it down, and there on the video screen was Anna Litical, the ACME CrimeLab director.

"Interesting thread you sent us," she said to Ben without so much as a hello. "Not much of it made in the U.S. Cheap stuff."

"Do you know if any of it is made near New Orleans?" Ben asked her.

"Let me search my database," said Anna. "Yes, there's one factory. They make cloth there too, lucky you. It's in Metairie, just outside New Orleans. Here's the number." She rattled off a phone number as Ben madly punched it into the computer.

"Thanks a lot, Anna," Ben said, but she had already signed off. All business, that one.

"It's strange that it's cheap thread," said Maya. "Carmen herself would never ever wear anything that wasn't top quality. If there's one thing she is, it's classy."

"You're right," said Ben. "That just reinforces your idea that Carmen's not here at all. She's probably just sending us on a wild-goose chase after one of her henchpeople."

"All we can do is hope the thread will lead us to Carmen and the colors from the Painted Desert," said Maya.

They tried the number of the factory right away, hoping someone might be there after hours, but they got no answer. "We're just silly to think anybody would be working on the last evening of Carnival." Maya sighed. "We'll have to stay over and start trying to track it down in the morning."

Tracking down a hotel room was the first order of business, and it was about as hard as finding Carmen Sandiego. It seemed as if every room in town was booked for the holiday. Finally they trudged wearily into the lobby of a small hotel at the edge of the French Quarter and asked the clerk if he had a room.

"You're in luck," he said. "Somebody just checked out of our junior suite early."

Maya and Ben had never been so happy to see a pair of bunk beds. They went downstairs, ordered some jambalaya for dinner, and happily scarfed up

49

the hot and spicy meat, vegetables, and rice. As they ate, they listened to the sounds of the police clearing the streets of people. It was midnight, and the great party was over. Then Ben and Maya went right to sleep.

Early the next morning, they got to work on the phone. First Maya called the factory, and asked if they had filled any unusual orders for fabric from the red thread lately.

"Let me see," said the owner's secretary. "Yes, here it is. I thought so. We had a special order from a tailor, right on Bourbon Street in New Orleans."

"Would you have the tailor's number?" Maya asked.

"I sure do, darlin'," said the woman. She read it off for Maya.

"Thanks a lot!" said Maya.

Next she called the tailor, Mr. Verlaine.

"I sure do remember that order," he said. "It was a big rush. I had to make forty of these red outfits, complete with hats, and I had only three days to get them finished. Let me tell you, I had people working here around the clock. The customer paid

50

quite a fee for them, though. I remember thinking that it was funny that they'd be willing to pay so much, when the material was so cheap."

"Could you tell me who the customer was?"

"That's the funny thing," said Mr. Verlaine. "I never got to find out. The money was dropped in my mail slot, cash, and then I had to leave the outfits outside the door of a room at the Hotel Excelsior in the Garden District. This was just the night before last. That was it. Never heard from the customer again."

"Do you remember what room number it was?"

"Clear as a bell. Room 305."

"Thanks, Mr. Verlaine. You've been really helpful."

"No problem."

Ben and Maya checked out of their hotel in ten minutes flat, and in another ten they were in the beautiful Garden District, looking for the Hotel Excelsior. It was a big, fancy old building with an old-fashioned cage elevator in the lobby.

Ben spoke to the woman at the desk. "We're trying to find the person who was registered here night before last, in room 305," he said.

"I'm afraid that person is long gone," she said.

51

"Checked out late last night, right around midnight."

"Can you tell me his or her name?" Ben asked.

"Why do you want to know?" she asked him, suddenly on her guard.

Ben fished out his official ACME badge and flashed it at her.

"What is that, some kind of a toy?" she said.

Ben was injured. "I assure you, madam, it is not," he said.

The woman kept standing there with her hands on her hips. She was definitely somebody's mother.

"Show her the Sender," Maya whispered to him.

Ben whipped the Sender out of his pocket. "Does *this* look like a toy?" he demanded.

"Well, yes," she said.

He sighed, flipped down the phone receiver, and dialed Yul.

"ACME Travel," said Yul, coming in on the video screen. "Hi, Ben."

"Hi, Yul," said Ben. "Sorry to bother you. I just needed you for proof."

"No problem," said Yul. "Talk to you soon."

"There," said Ben to the woman.

"Well, that certainly looks real," she conceded.

"But I'm still not sure how much I can help you."

"All we need is the name of the person who was in 305."

She opened her guest book and turned to Monday's page. "Oh, here it is. 'J. Smith.'" She snorted. "*That's* original," she said.

"Do you know if it was a man or a woman?" Maya asked.

"You know, it's funny. I couldn't tell. He or she had on a baseball cap, no hair down, and a windbreaker with the collar turned all the way up. Didn't even talk, just signed in."

"Did this person pay with a credit card?"

"Nope. Straight cash."

"Rats," said Ben.

"Could we see room 305?" Maya inquired.

"I don't see why not," said the woman. "Though I don't think you'll find much up there. The room's been cleaned already." She handed Maya the key and pointed toward the elevator. "Third floor, end of the hall," she said.

As they were crossing the lobby, the woman called out to them. "One little item I just remembered," she said. "The funniest thing."

The two kids turned.

53

"The whole time the person in 305 was here, he or she kept ordering in French food. Only French. Not that we don't have great French food here in New Orleans, but we're famous for our Creole and Cajun food too. But this person just kept ordering French—French for breakfast, French for lunch, French for dinner."

Ben broke into a wide grin. "Thanks!" he said. "That's a bigger help than you know."

They let themselves into room 305, which was, as expected, clean and tidy. "We probably won't find much here," said Maya.

They poked around, but the ashtrays and wastebaskets were cleaned out. Nothing under the bed. Nothing left in the closets.

Ben plopped down on the bed while Maya continued nosing around the room. "Maybe I'll pull up those dossiers again and see who likes French food," he said.

"Good idea," Maya agreed.

"Okay," said Ben, pushing buttons. "Let's see. We were right about Freda D. Darke. It wasn't her—she likes Italian food. Liza Lotsa's a possibility—she likes French food. So does Dee Molish. Aha—Armand Geddon also likes French food.

Hugo Yurway's a vegetarian, and Nell N. Void likes French. I think that's everybody who was in the Southwest."

"Can you run that down for me again? Who likes French food?"

Ben checked again. "Liza Lotsa. Dee Molish. Armand Geddon. Nell N. Void."

"Well, that knocks out a couple of them, anyhow. It's a good start."

Maya idly opened the refrigerator and peered into the little freezer on top. "Hey, what's this?" she exclaimed.

She pulled two small objects out of the freezer.

Ben stood up. "What'd you find?" he asked her.

"They're beautiful," said Maya. "They're some kind of little ice sculptures."

"They're in the shape of tiny cities," said Ben.

"And they're exactly the same," Maya remarked.

"Hmmm," said Ben.

"Hmmm," said Maya.

"Twin cities!" they shouted together.

"What are the Twin Cities?" Ben asked. "I can't remember. New York and New Jersey?"

"New Jersey's a *state*, doofus," said Maya.

"The Twin Cities are in Minnesota. Minneapolis and St. Paul."

"I knew that," said Ben.

"It's funny that those little sculptures were left in the freezer," said Maya thoughtfully. "Almost as if they were left there on purpose."

"For us? To lead us to the next place?"

"Well, you have to admit, it is funny, isn't it?"

"I guess it is," said Ben. "But funny or not, I'd better call Yul back. We have to see if we can find Liza or Dee or Armand or Nell in Minnesota."

Yul appeared, smiling on the video screen. "You missed me, huh?" he said.

Ben told him they needed some transportation to the Twin Cities.

"That's a great choice," said Yul. "Fun stuff going on there now. Late February is when they have their big winter carnival. Terrific ice sculptures."

"Bingo," said Maya.

6
Minneapolis, Minnesota

In one hour, Ben and Maya were standing at the end of the Canal Street wharf, on the Mississippi River. Yul had told them to wait there. "This one's easy," he'd said. "We'll just zip you right up the river, straight to Minnesota."

"You mean, the river goes all the way up there?" Ben had asked.

"It *starts* all the way up there, my little pumpernickel," Yul had replied. "In Itaska, to be exact. Anyhow, I've got a special little test vehicle I've been waiting to try out. River hovercraft. Get you there in no time."

Maya looked up and down the river. "Where

the heck is it?" she fussed. "The trail will get cold if we don't get up there."

At that moment, the kids heard a loud buzzing sound from the left. They craned their necks to see what was coming around the bend. And then it appeared: a little bright-red hovercraft, just big enough for two people. It skimmed above the surface of the water, kept aloft by strong jets of air from its underside. Painted on its bow were the words *Bayou Belle*.

"Oh, it's so adorable!" said Maya.

"Yeah, it's cute, but I don't think it's going to stop," Ben said, watching it zipping toward them without slowing down.

"That's okay, we'll just jump into it when it gets here," said Maya cheerfully.

"Easy for you to say," grumbled Ben.

"Okay—one, two, three, *go!*"

"I don't want tooooo!" yelled Ben as they both leaped into the boat.

When they had scrambled onto the seats, Maya began checking the controls.

Ben rubbed a sore knee. "I'm tired of Yul sending us things that don't stop for us to get on or off," he said.

"I think he's done pretty well. He hasn't had much to work with," said Maya.

"I guess you're right." And in fact, the little hovercraft was skimming up the river at a very good clip.

"Let's call him and find out how this thing works," said Maya. Ben handed her the Sender, and in a minute Yul was on the screen.

"So, my little sugarplums, you like my new test vehicle?"

"It's great," said Maya. "But how do we work it?"

"I've got all the controls preset," Yul explained. "It's on autopilot, so you don't have to do a thing. I'll be watching you from here, and I'll use my computer guidance system to get you through any rough spots. I'll have one of our operatives meet you up in Minnesota and take the boat from you. You can go to sleep if you feel like it."

And in about half an hour, when they were out of New Orleans, they did feel like it. The sun was beating down, the air was muggy, and the bugs were buzzing. Ben and Maya both drifted off as the boat carried them northward.

Some time later, Maya stirred to find Ben on

his knees, taking something out of a box beneath the seat. She rubbed her eyes. "Where are we?" she asked.

"We're passing through St. Louis, Missouri."

She sat up. "You're right!" she said. "Look! There's the Gateway Arch!" Just ahead, to their left, was a huge, gleaming silver arch that soared gracefully into the sky.

"Even I know that the arch means we're in St. Louis," said Ben.

Maya pulled her shirt tighter around her. "I'm cold," she said.

"I know," said Ben. "We've come pretty far north, and we have a lot farther to go. Here," he said, holding something big and green out to her. "I found a blanket in the box. We can get under it."

They huddled under the warm blanket for the rest of the day, watching Missouri and Iowa go by on their left, Illinois and Wisconsin on their right. The air got colder and colder, and Ben and Maya scooted farther and farther down under the cover.

At last, as evening fell, they reached the Twin Cities. The river wasn't as wide here, but it was still full of boat traffic. Several bridges spanned the water, connecting Minneapolis and St. Paul.

"Holy cow!" said Ben. "What's that?"

There, straight ahead of them, was the most incredible thing. It was a huge castle made of ice, lit up with colored lights. It soared fifteen stories into the air, all pointed towers and flags.

"Unbelievable," said Maya.

The hovercraft began slowing down by itself as it approached the end of a pier, where a man was standing and waving his arms at them. The boat stopped right at his feet.

"What a nice change," Ben said to Maya, his teeth chattering.

The man reached his arms down to pull the kids up. "Herbert Heeberg, at your service," he said as they climbed onto the pier. "Yul sent me to meet you. He suggested I bring these." He bent over and began handing them things from a pile of items on the pier beside him: Parkas! Mittens! Hats! Ben and Maya had never been so happy to see warm clothes in their lives.

"I'll take the hovercraft from here," said Herbert. "I have to send it back to Yul."

"Before you go," said Maya, "can you tell us something about that ice castle?"

"For sure," Herbert replied. "That's the crowning glory of the Winter Carnival. They cut huge chunks right out of the river to make the ice sculptures. Some of them weigh seven hundred pounds. Have to use chain saws. If you walk around, you'll see lots of other sculptures too."

"That's great," said Maya. "We will."

Herbert got into the boat and zoomed off, waving.

"Now," said Ben, feeling a lot warmer, "we just have to figure out what we're looking for."

"Until we do," said Maya, "we might as well walk around and look at this stuff."

They joined the happy crowds looking at all the ice sculptures. There were swans and eagles, dragons and angels. Everything was beautiful.

There was a big crowd around a sculpture some distance away. It was in the shape of a great big ring, with a tremendous chunk of ice cut like a precious stone. The stone was lit all the way through with a beautiful green light so that it sparkled like an emerald. Someone in a big furry brown parka was tapping away at the top of the sculpture with a chisel and hammer.

Ben and Maya got closer to take a better look.

"Hey," said Maya. "Ben, look at this." He leaned over to see what she was pointing at.

A small plaque was affixed to the front of the sculpture. THIS SCULPTURE DONATED BY C. SANDIEGO, it read.

"Good grief!" Ben exclaimed. "It's whoever we're chasing!"

Maya cupped her hands and shouted up to the person on the top. "Hello! Up there! We'd like to talk to you!"

The person in the parka glanced down at Ben and Maya, and then took off, sliding down the far side of the ring and landing with a thump. Ben and Maya immediately gave chase. "Stop!" yelled Maya. "We need to talk to you about the Painted Desert!"

People were looking at them very strangely, but Maya and Ben kept running after the figure, who was hurtling through the crowd, elbowing people out of the way. Fifty other furry brown parkas in the crowd didn't help matters any.

Just up ahead was the huge ice castle. Carmen's henchperson probably thought he or she could lose Ben and Maya there, but the two kids were determined not to let it happen. It was slow going

64

through the crowd, though, especially since the kids weren't about to push and shove people the way their suspect did.

"There!" cried Maya as they got to the castle. "Look!" The kids raced after the receding figure, who had already entered the lit-up castle.

Inside, they suddenly found themselves in another world. It was strangely quiet and windless, with the translucent blocks of ice glowing pink and blue and orange all around them. The fleeing figure was nowhere to be seen.

"You go to the left," said Maya. "I'll go around to the right."

"Okay," said Ben.

They ran through the whole castle, finally meeting again outside. But they'd failed.

"Rats!" said Ben. "Lost him!"

"Or her," said Maya. "Maybe we should go back to that ring sculpture. Just to see."

They ran through the crowd again, back to the emerald ring. The crowd was still there, but the figure in the furry parka was not.

Beside the ring sculpture, a man with a beard was using an ice pick to put the finishing touches on a beautiful sculpture of two angels with trumpets.

"Excuse me," Maya said to the man. "But do you know anything about the person who was building the emerald ring sculpture next door?"

"Well, I talked to her a couple of times," said the man.

Her! Ben and Maya exchanged excited glances.

"What did she say?" Ben asked.

"She said she would be going to New York tomorrow. Which is really too bad, because they're going to judge the sculptures tomorrow, and she won't be here to see if she won. But she said she had to be in New York, and it has to be tomorrow, because she's going to the opening of her exhibition."

"Exhibition?"

"Yeah." He chuckled. "It's the darnedest thing. She said she's having a show of her paint-by-number clown pictures. Said that sort of thing is really big in New York now. I guess they'll swallow anything back East." He laughed again.

"Can I ask you a question?" said Maya. "What did she look like? What color hair did she have? What color eyes?"

"I really couldn't see much of her," said the man. "She had that furry parka hood pulled tight,

66

so only a little of her face showed. I couldn't see her hair at all. I couldn't see her eyes, either—she had sunglasses on. Why do you want to know, anyway? Is she a friend of yours?"

"We're hoping she is. An old friend," Maya lied. "We wanted to surprise her."

"Well, good luck finding her," said the man, turning back to his sculpture.

Ben and Maya took one last turn around the sculpture area, hoping to spot her. But she'd taken off.

"I guess we're going to New York," said Ben.

7

Somewhere Over
the Eastern U.S.,
Altitude 30,000 Feet

This time Yul was able to put them on a regular flight to New York City. They had only been in Minnesota for a few hours, so their flight left very late that same night. It was scheduled to get into New York early in the morning. The lights in the plane were turned down low, and most of the travelers were sleeping under their meager little airline blankets. Ben and Maya were awake, though. Awake and thinking.

"Okay," said Maya. "What do we know?"

"We knew this morning that it was Liza Lotsa,

or Dee Molish, or Armand Geddon, or Nell N. Void," said Ben, "because they are the only ones who like French food. And now we know it can't be Armand, because the man in Minneapolis said it was a woman."

Maya furrowed her brows. "Clown paintings," she said. "Why does that ring a bell?"

"It sounds familiar to me too," said Ben. "Let's pull up the dossiers."

He got out the Sender and punched in the codes to get the dossiers up on the screen again.

"Aha!" he said. "There it is! It's Dee Molish! She's our culprit!"

Maya leaned over to look, and there it was, all right. Dee Molish loved doing paint-by-number clown pictures.

"It makes sense," said Ben. "Maybe she's using the colors from the Painted Desert for her paintings or something."

"Let's call Wanda and order a warrant for Dee," said Maya. "Then when we find her in New York, at the clown-painting exhibition, bang! We'll arrest her."

"Okay," said Ben. "But first I think we'd better

give The Chief a call and tell her where we really are. I don't like pretending, and she's got to know sometime."

"You're right," said Maya. "Just hold your ears when you tell her."

"I thought maybe you'd tell her," said Ben, grimacing.

Just then the Sender beeped. It was the special high-pitched beep reserved for calls coming in to the office on the red phone. Ben answered it.

"Howdy, Ben," said a familiar voice. (The Sender's video hookup didn't work with calls on the red phone.) "It's Loco."

"Loco!" said Ben. "Are you okay? What's happened?"

"I'm fine," said Loco. "Everything's about the same here—black and white. It's driving me a little nuts, if you want to know the truth. But listen, there's a friend of mine here, and I think you should talk to him. He's a scientist here in the desert. Studies snakes and lizards, mostly. Name's Dr. Herbie Tologist. I'm going to put him on. Here you go, Herbie."

A new voice came on the line.

70

"Hi," said Herbie. "I'm glad to talk to you, and I hope you're making some progress with getting the colors back into the desert. There's a very big problem here, you see."

"What is it?" Ben asked.

"It's about the Painted Desert glossy snake," Dr. Tologist explained. "Very nice snake, too. It's important in the food chain here. It feeds a lot of birds and rodents and such."

"And what's happened to it?"

"Well, it's about what's going to happen. It's about to become extinct. You see, this particular species of snake is perfectly camouflaged. It's colored exactly to match its surroundings here in the Painted Desert. Except now the desert is black and white. That means the snake sticks out like a sore thumb, and they're getting picked off by the hundreds. They'll all be gone soon. And that's bad news for the whole desert ecosystem, not just the Painted Desert glossy snake."

"Jeepers creepers," said Ben. "That's awful."

"It sure is," said the scientist. "Life is hard enough in the desert without this happening."

"Dr. Tologist, we're working as hard as we can

to figure out who did this thing. I think we'll have it solved pretty soon."

"I sure hope so," said Dr. Tologist.

Ben signed off. "Whoo," he said. "This adds a whole new problem." He explained the situation to Maya.

"It's a good thing we figured out that it's Dee Molish," she said. "We can have this whole case wrapped up in a day or two, and then the colors will go back where they belong."

"Let's call The Chief now," said Ben.

"You mean, let's *me* call The Chief now." Maya reached for the Sender. "She's my aunt," she said. "Maybe she has a rule about not firing a relative."

She dialed the secret number, and in a moment The Chief appeared on the Sender's screen. She looked pretty grouchy even before Maya started talking.

"Um, hi, Chief," said Maya.

"How are you two doing back there?" asked The Chief.

Maya swallowed hard and then told The Chief everything.

There was a long pause. Then The Chief cleared

her throat. "I . . . am . . . not . . . happy," she said at last.

"I know, Chief," said Maya. "And we're really sorry. But we thought if we told you, you wouldn't have let us go at all, and then nobody would be saving the Painted Desert."

"You're probably right," said The Chief with a sigh. "I'm sure I wouldn't have let you go."

"So, can we keep going?"

The Chief sighed once again. "Just don't screw it up," she said. "Because if you do, you're going to be demoted to Assistant Assistant Gumshoe."

"Chief, does that position exist?"

"We're going to create it, just for you," she replied. "Now keep me posted as to your where-abouts."

"Right, Chief. Definitely, Chief."

Maya signed off, looking unhappy. "We'd better have this right," she said.

"I don't see how we could be wrong," said Ben. "We know the person likes French food, is a woman, and paints clowns. It has to be Dee."

"Okay, let's call Wanda and order the warrant," said Maya.

They called Wanda the Warrant Officer, who appeared on the video screen in her little ACME uniform and hat. "What'll it be?" she asked.

They told her what they wanted.

"You sure?" she asked, popping her bubble gum.

"We're sure," they said.

"Okay, you got it. It'll come through on the Sender later on today."

"Thanks, Wanda."

The plane was about to land in New York. In the predawn dark, the Manhattan skyline was beautiful, with the twin towers of the World Trade Center downtown, and the pointed top of the Empire State Building farther north.

Ben and Maya were really tired, since they hadn't slept all night. They decided to check into a hotel, catch a couple hours of sleep, and then look for Dee. It was too early to do much anyhow.

Drat! Cut off at the pass—and just when every-thing was going according to plan. It's a good thing I've figured out how to tap into the CrimeNet, or I wouldn't have heard about this snake prob-lem. Well, of course, we can't let that happen. I wouldn't dream of making any species extinct. This just means I have more reason to make sure my original plan works. I've got to lead those rook-ies to the stolen colors. I won't make it too easy, of course—they've got to figure it out for them-selves. But they'll have to get the colors back, and sooner rather than later.

8

Empire State Building, New York City

When they got up at nine-thirty, the first thing Ben and Maya did was go down to the hotel lobby, buy a *New York Times*, and head for the coffee shop to get some breakfast. They opened the paper as they drank their orange juice.

"Look in the arts section," Maya told Ben. "See where the opening for the paint-by-number clown exhibition is being held."

Ben looked, and then he looked some more. "I can't find an ad for the gallery," he said.

"Maybe it's at a museum."

Ben kept looking. "Nothing."

Maya looked over his shoulder. "Here's something," she said, pointing. " 'Arts Line.' We can call it and find out what's happening anywhere in the city."

She fished a quarter out of her pocket, walked to the pay phone in the corner of the coffee shop, and dialed the number.

"I'm looking for the gallery that's having the exhibition of paint-by-number clowns," she told the woman who answered.

There was a snort on the other end. "Paint-by-number *whats*?"

"Clowns."

"Dear, I'm afraid you're sadly mistaken. This is the Arts Line, not the Tasteless Junk Line. There isn't a gallery in all of New York that would be so tacky. If you want to find an exhibit of paint-by-number clowns, I suggest you look in your great-aunt's basement."

New Yorkers could be so harsh.

Maya shuffled back to the booth, where Ben was just digging into his fried eggs. "No luck," she said. "There's no paint-by-number clown exhibition."

Ben was alarmed. "But Dee said—"

"I know," Maya replied. "Maybe the ice sculptor guy didn't hear her right. Or maybe it's at some little, extremely cool gallery downtown that the Arts Line doesn't know about."

"What do we do now?" Ben wondered. "We were going to nab her at this opening."

"I have an idea. We have a crackerjack undercover informant in New York—I've heard The Chief mention him several times. His name's Professor Bob."

"Oh, yeah, I've heard her talk about him too."

"Let's see if we can contact him on the Sender," suggested Maya.

Ben consulted the data bank in the Sender's computer to find out the code for reaching Professor Bob. Then he punched it in.

In seconds, Professor Bob appeared on the video screen. His face was covered with sweat, he was breathing hard, and he appeared to be running even while he talked on the Sender.

Ben introduced himself and Maya, and asked if Professor Bob might be able to help them find Dee Molish.

"It just so happens," panted Professor Bob, "that I'm trailing her at this very minute. I caught sight

78

of her on the Staten Island Ferry, and I decided to see what she was up to. Nothing legal, I'm sure."

Ben could hardly believe their good fortune. "Where are you now, Professor Bob?" he asked.

"She's whizzing up Fifth Avenue on in-line skates" was the reply. "Against traffic, I might add. I'm right behind her on a skateboard I borrowed from a kid. We're at about Fourteenth Street."

"Okay, I'll tell you what," said Ben, thinking fast. "We'll jump into a taxicab and head toward Fifth Avenue, and we'll keep in touch with you. Maybe we can meet you."

"All right," puffed Professor Bob. "I just hope I don't lose her."

Ben and Maya hurriedly paid for their breakfast, Maya grabbed her bagel, and they ran. In the street they flagged down a yellow cab. "Fifth Avenue, please," said Maya.

"Where on Fifth Avenue?" inquired the cabdriver, a young woman with spiky hair and a gold ring in her nose.

"We're not sure yet," said Maya. "Head downtown. We'll tell you when we get there."

"Okay by me," said the driver. She stepped on the gas.

When they got to Fifth Avenue and Seventy-second Street, Ben dialed Professor Bob again. "How's it going?" he asked.

"I'm . . . still . . . with her," panted Professor Bob. "We're just about to enter the Empire State Building, on Thirty-fourth Street. There's a big crowd here—something unusual is going on. Wait a second, there's a banner." He looked to the right, panting. "It's the Empire State Building Run-Up."

"What's that?" asked Ben.

"Annual race up the Empire State Building. I think . . ." gasped Professor Bob, "that these people are crazy."

"What's Dee doing?" asked Ben.

"She's signing up," was the reply.

"We'll be right there," said Ben.

"Okay, now we know where we're going," Maya said to the cabdriver. "The Empire State Building—and step on it."

Their cabdriver wove expertly through the midtown traffic, and they arrived at the Empire State Building in no time flat. Ben and Maya paid and jumped out of the cab.

The building's huge lobby was filled with

people—contestants in running shorts, officials, onlookers, and confused tourists.

"I can't believe this," said Maya. "These people are going to run a race *up* the Empire State Building?"

Ben was reading a sign in the lobby. "It looks that way," he said. "They run up eighty-six flights of stairs to the observation deck. King Kong is there to greet the winner, the sign says."

"Boy, oh boy," said Maya. "What will they think of next?"

"Look!" said Ben. "There's Dee!"

Sure enough, there she was, still in her skates, wearing her number 12 Roller Derby jersey. She was elbowing people out of the way, trying to get to the front of the starting pack.

"Hey!" somebody yelped. "Those elbows are sharp!"

A man stepped up to Maya and Ben. "ACME?" he said.

"ACME," said Ben. "Thanks for the help, Professor Bob. You were great."

"There she goes!" said Maya. "They're starting up!"

"I think," said Professor Bob, who was still

breathing hard, "that I won't go up, if you don't mind."

"We can take it from here," said Ben.

"I'll wait down in the lobby," said Professor Bob.

The kids took off after Dee, who was clomping up the stairs at a great pace in her skates. There were about a hundred people between the kids and Dee.

Up the staircase they went. One flight. Two flights. Ten flights. Twenty flights. "It's a good thing we've gotten all that ACME fitness training," panted Ben.

"Yeah. I think I should have done more jogging," Maya panted back.

Forty flights. Sixty flights. Their lungs were on fire, but they were gaining on Dee, who was near the front of the pack.

The Sender beeped, and Ben unfolded it without missing a step. It was the warrant from Wanda, coming through electronically.

"Good," said Maya. "Now we can arrest her when we get to the top."

Seventy flights. Seventy-five. Ben and Maya thought they were going to die.

At last they were almost there. Incredibly, the

whole climb had taken only about eleven minutes. And there, waiting at the top, was King Kong, stretching out his hairy paw to Dee.

"Dee Molish," yelled Ben, "you are under arrest!"

Dee turned to look at them. She looked wide-eyed and innocent.

"Whatever for?" she asked, flashing them a gap-toothed grin.

"You know what for," said Maya. All the other runners had stopped to watch in disbelief.

"No, I *don't* know what for," she said. King Kong by this time had his hands on his hips and was tapping his large, hairy foot.

"For the theft of the colors from the Painted Desert," said Ben. "You have the right to remain silent—"

"Silent? I don't think so!" said Dee. "When did this *supposed* theft happen, anyway?"

"Four days ago," said Ben.

"Well, as it happens," gloated Dee, "I couldn't have stolen any colors from anywhere."

"Why not?" Maya asked.

"Because," said Dee triumphantly, "I was in jail. And they only have black-and-white stripes in

there!" She danced a little jig in her skates. "I went in two weeks ago. Just got out this morning."

Ben and Maya were stricken. How could this possibly be? There must be some mistake.

"Hold it right there," Ben said to Dee. "I have to check your story." He dialed up the ACME CrimeNet, which patched him through to the Twenty-fifth Precinct in New York.

"Yeah," said the cop when Ben asked him about Dee. "She was in jail, all right. We were all happy to see her go."

"What was she arrested for?"

"She was in the Metropolitan Museum. We nabbed her taking down a Rembrandt and putting up a paint-by-number picture of a clown instead. She kept talking about how 'true genius is never recognized' or some such."

"Oh, brother," said Ben.

"Now," said Dee, "you *have* to let me go. Ha ha ha!" She turned to King Kong. "Now gimme that prize," she demanded.

"Sorry," said King Kong in a muffled voice through his costume. "People on skates are disqualified. And you two kids would have won—if you had registered. Too bad." He shook hands with the woman right behind Dee, and handed her a trophy.

"Hey, wait a second!" yelled Dee.

"Just don't damage the stairs with your skates on the way down," said King Kong.

There was a reception at the top of the Empire State Building for all the contestants, but Ben and Maya were in no mood for a party. Dee had already disappeared into the crowd, grumbling about losing her prize.

The kids trudged wearily down the stairs, trying to figure out what had gone wrong.

"How could we have come all this way for nothing?" moaned Maya.

"How could we have gotten a warrant for the wrong person?" Ben moaned back. "This is going to make us look so bad. Really bad."

In the lobby, Professor Bob was still waiting for them. He looked a lot better now.

"Why so glum?" he asked them. "You caught her, right?"

"We caught her, all right," said Ben. "But she was the wrong person. We got a warrant for nothing."

Professor Bob looked concerned. "That's too bad," he said.

The kids were so depressed, they couldn't speak.

"But you know," Professor Bob went on, "mistakes are golden opportunities, I always say. Mistakes are great chances to learn."

No wonder they called him Professor Bob. It was just like a teacher to say something like that.

"Yeah," said Maya. "We learned that we're Assistant Assistant Gumshoes."

"Not at all. Not at all," said Professor Bob. "You just learned that things aren't always as they seem. I've had lots of wrong warrants issued in my time. What you do when that happens is, you go back and look at all your facts. You'll figure out where you went wrong. Just look at your facts."

Ben and Maya started feeling a little hopeful. "You've really gotten wrong warrants before?"

"Certainly. Once I followed Nick Brunch all the way to Turkey, only to find out that the real culprit was Katherine Drib, who was calmly *eating* some turkey in Costa Rica."

"Wow."

"So, if I were you," said Professor Bob, "I'd hole up somewhere for a little while, get out all your dossiers, and think things through over and over, until you get the right answer. Now I've got to go return this skateboard."

The kids said a grateful good-bye to Professor Bob, and decided to do just as he had suggested. They'd go back to their hotel room and review all the facts again.

"Just do me a favor," Maya said to Ben as they walked up Madison Avenue toward their hotel.

"What's that?"

"Turn off the beeper on the Sender. I don't want to talk to The Chief when she calls."

9
New York, New York

For the next twenty-four hours, Ben and Maya
sat in their hotel suite and went over and over
the case, taking short breaks for sleep. They were
completely stymied. Could Dee somehow have
stolen the colors while she was in jail? It was hard
to figure out how, and besides, there was that
notepad in the shack in the desert. A real person
had left that note. But who?

Or maybe the man making the angel sculpture
had been mistaken about what his neighbor had
said about going to New York. But how could anybody make up something as ridiculous as an exhibition of paint-by-number clowns?

They even considered the possibility that the
angel sculptor was a V.I.L.E. operative. But they

pulled up the dossier of every known V.I.L.E. agent worldwide, even galaxy-wide, and none of them matched. Besides, the man was just too nice and normal to be a V.I.L.E. agent. V.I.L.E. agents were all peculiar. Carmen seemed to like them that way.

After staring at the dossiers for hours and hours, Ben finally gave up and turned on the beeper. Even if Maya couldn't face The Chief, they really needed her help.

Almost immediately, The Chief called. Ben answered the beep.

"So," said The Chief. "I heard about your false warrant. Very impressive detective work."

"Sorry, Chief," said Ben. "We really thought it was Dee. Everything pointed to her. Honest."

The Chief just sighed a deep and exasperated sigh.

"Uh, Chief?" Ben asked meekly.

"What?"

"Are we still on the case?"

"Yes, you're still on the case. Somebody has to figure out who stole the colors from the Painted Desert. That part, at least, you're right about—my reports confirm it. And you're the only agents who

90

are free now. The rest of us are still stuck on the date line, waiting for something to happen. Although I'm beginning to suspect that the whole thing's a gigantic red herring."

"What's a red herring?" Maya asked.

"Something to throw us off the scent of the real crime. A diversion."

"Oh. Thanks, Chief," said Maya.

"The CrimeNet keeps telling us to watch the date line, but everything's awfully quiet up and down the whole length of it. I'm starting to think maybe our intelligence is screwy."

"Gosh, I hope not," said Ben.

"Anyhow, you might as well keep working on this case. Go back over your clues and see where your mistake is."

"Right, Chief," said Ben.

"And eat some vegetables!"

"We sure will, Chief. 'Bye, Chief."

Ben hung up. "Maybe we'd better go down to the coffee shop and order some broccoli," he said to Maya.

They put their shoes on and went downstairs. Ben ordered broccoli and Maya ordered string beans. They were the first vegetables that had crossed their lips in a few days.

"So," said Maya, stuffing a bean into her mouth, "we knew for sure that the culprit liked French food, because of what the clerk said in the hotel in New Orleans. Right?"

"Right," said Ben. They'd been over this about a hundred times already.

"So, that put Freda D. Darke and Hugo Yurway out of the running. Right?"

"Right."

"And we found out that it was a woman, so that eliminated Armand Geddon. Right?"

"Right."

"So," said Maya, eating her last bean, "that left us with Liza Lotsa, Nell N. Void, and Dee Molish. And then we found out that the culprit was going to New York for a clown-painting exhibition, and that absolutely had to be Dee. Right?"

"Right. Except it wasn't Dee."

They paid their bill and went back upstairs to their by now very messy room.

"Let's just pull up the dossiers on Dee, Liza, and Nell again," said Maya. "Maybe there's something there we missed."

Ben opened the Sender and pulled up the dossiers. They pored over them, as they had twenty times before.

Suddenly Maya smacked her forehead. "I've got it," she said.

"You do?"

"Yup. It's right here in front of our eyes. What if," she said, "what if the guy who was sculpting the angels wasn't told the truth?"

"Howzat?"

"Take a look here," she said, pointing to a dossier on the Sender's screen.

"'Liza Lotsa,'" Ben read. "'Lotsa likes French food, stargazing, skiing, classical music. Fancy schmancy, likes yachts and Rolls-Royces. Tells tall tales and white lies.'"

He jumped to his bare feet. "She lies!" he yelled. "Maybe she lied to the sculptor about the clown paintings!"

"Exactly," said Maya. "And look at this." She pointed a little farther down on the screen.

"Emeralds!" shouted Ben. "She loves emeralds! And that's what her sculpture was—an emerald ring!"

"Bingo," said Maya.

"Now all we have to do is figure out where to

find her," said Ben. "We lost her back in St. Paul, when she sent us on this wild-goose chase to New York."

"Maybe we should get Wanda started on a warrant for her, while we figure out how to find her," said Maya. "We don't want her to get away when we get hold of her."

"I don't know," said Ben doubtfully. "Look what happened last time. I think we should wait with the warrant, until we know for sure. Maybe we missed something else, or figured it out wrong again. Maybe it's Nell N. Void. Or maybe it's the man in the moon. I don't want to swear out a false warrant again. Once is enough for me."

"Okay, okay. But I'm sure it's Liza."

There was a knock on the door. Ben and Maya looked at each other, wondering who on earth it could be. They certainly weren't expecting anybody.

Maya went to the door. "Who is it?" she asked.

"Room service," said a male voice.

Maya looked through the peephole in the door. There, distorted through the fish-eye lens, was a waiter in a hotel uniform, with a hotel cart.

"Should we let him in?" she whispered to Ben.

Ben shrugged helplessly.

Maya talked through the door. "We didn't order any room service," she said.

"This is compliments of the management," said the waiter.

Ben and Maya looked at each other again, and then Maya opened the door. A very short man with a mustache wheeled in the cart, stopped in the middle of the room, and gave a little bow.

Maya very, very carefully lifted the stainless steel dome that covered one of the dishes. On the dish were two tall, frosty glasses of milk.

A smaller dome covered the other dish, and Maya peeked under that one next. "Fortune cookies!" she cried. "There's one for each of us!"

"Whew," said Ben. "That was scary."

Maya turned to the waiter. "Thanks," she said. She waited for him to go. Instead, he cleared his throat.

Ben cupped his hands to Maya's ear. "We're supposed to tip him," he whispered.

"Ooooh," said Maya, getting it. She dug in the pocket of her jeans and found two quarters, and handed them to the waiter. He looked at the coins with some distaste before he turned and left.

"Well, gosh," said Maya indignantly.

Ben and Maya sat on the edge of Maya's bed to eat their bedtime snack. They were glad to have this little gift from the management, because they hadn't remembered to eat much today except for the vegetables in the coffee shop. Ben broke open his fortune cookie eagerly.

"Hey," he said, puzzling over the little strip of paper inside it. "This fortune doesn't make any sense."

Maya leaned over to look at Ben's fortune. It said: 112°W.

"Weird," she said. "Must be a misprint." Then she broke open her own cookie.

"Huh?" She stared at the fortune. It said: 41°N.

"What the heck is this?" Ben wondered aloud.

"Yeah, I expected 'He who hesitates is lost' or something. What good are a bunch of numbers?"

Ben balled up his fortune into a tiny pellet and flicked it across the room into the wastebasket. "Two points!" he crowed.

"Wait, hold on," said Maya, suddenly intense. "Get that back, will you?"

"Huh?" said Ben. But he knew better than to argue with Maya. He walked over and took the little wad out of the wastebasket, and handed it to her. She smoothed it out on the bedspread, beside her own.

"What do these look like to you?" she asked him.

"A couple of useless fortunes," Ben said.

"Nope. You know what they are? They're map coordinates. Latitude and longitude. Look: 112 degrees west, 41 degrees north. Somebody's telling us something!"

"The hotel manager?"

"I really doubt it," said Maya, opening the computer flap on the Sender. "It's somebody else, someone connected with this case."

She punched in the coordinates and waited for them to come up on the Sender's computer screen. It took only a second.

"The Great Salt Lake," she said. "Right near Salt Lake City, Utah."

"Wow," said Ben, flopping down on the bed.

"Now," said Maya, knitting her brows. "If we only knew whether it was somebody good or somebody bad who wanted us to go there."

"There's only one way to find out," said Ben.

Oh, I'm so pleased. My little plan is getting back on track now. Those young detectives have recovered nicely from their setback, and they'll be making real headway in no time. And no time is just about what we have, too, because the other ACME detectives are going to figure out very soon that I've sent them to the international date line for nothing. The Chief is already beginning to suspect that I've learned how to tap into the CrimeNet. Now, if everything works according to plan, those rookies will get the Painted Desert's colors back before any harm comes to that Painted Desert groggy snake, or whatever it's called.

Yes, I think this will all end up just fine. I'll have had some fun, which is always the basic point, and The Chief will appreciate her young detectives a little more. She doesn't realize how close they came to nabbing me last time. They're worthy adversaries, and she ought to give them a little more credit! That, of course, is why I'm contributing a bit of help along the way here, enough to keep them moving in the right direction. Just as long as they don't actually catch me, that is.

10
Salt Lake City, Utah

Ben and Maya took a train to Salt Lake City the next morning, because Ben was getting a cold and didn't want to fly with stuffy ears. Yul got them reservations in the sleeper car. They slept blissfully, with the sound of the rails clacking rhythmically in their ears and the motion of the train rocking them back and forth all night. In the daytime they watched the landscape change as it flew past them, and the weather got sunnier and hotter.

"It's probably just as well that we didn't pack for this trip," said Maya. "We would never have known what to take, with all the running around we've done since we left Headquarters. Hot, cold, hot, cold. It's been crazy."

At last, after fifty-two hours, the conductor announced that they were pulling into Salt Lake City.

"Have you given any thought to what we're going to do when we get there?" Ben asked Maya. "Just curious."

"I have no clue," said Maya cheerfully. "I thought we'd just head for the lake and see what happens. Somebody's watching us. We just have to wait and see who it is."

As the train ground to a halt, they stood up, stretched, and got their bags out of the overhead compartment. "I really don't want to drag this around with me now that it's warmer," said Ben, pulling down the plastic bag that contained his parka and mittens.

"Might as well take it," said Maya. "We don't know where we're going to end up."

They got off the train and stood amid the swirling crowd, looking for signs to tell them which way to go. But before they had a chance to decide, a businesslike figure approached them, clipping quickly along on high heels. She stopped in front of them, straightening the shoulder pads on her well-cut tweed suit.

"Nell N. Void," said the woman. "Let the record show that I am the party of the first part, arraigned in Spain for the current proceedings."

"Huh?" said Ben.

Maya whispered into his ear. "She used to be a big-time lawyer, remember? She talks lawyerese."

"In strict accordance with the writ of abeas-hay orpus-cay, and being of sound mind and body, I do solemnly present myself to you on my own recognizance."

"Abeas-hay what?" said Ben.

"Habeus corpus. She uses a lot of pig latin, too," Maya reminded him in a whisper.

"What the heck is she *talking* about?" Ben asked.

"I think she's turning herself in to us," Maya whispered.

Maya seemed to be right. Nell was sticking out her hands as if she wanted to be handcuffed.

"Remember, I have the ight-ray to remain silent. I have the ight-ray to an attorney, and if I cannot afford an attorney I have the ight-ray to have an attorney appointed by the court. . . ."

"Hold on a second," said Ben.

"Something's fishy here," said Maya, her eyes narrowed. "Why would she turn herself in, just like that?"

"I disrespectfully decline to answer on the grounds that I might incriminate myself."

"And what if we don't want to issue a warrant for your arrest?" said Maya. "What are you going to do about it?"

Nell looked taken aback. "Objection, Your Honor! That question is irrelevant, immaterial, and calls for a concussion on the part of the witness."

"This is ridiculous," said Ben. "I say let her go."

"Why, that would be against ocedure-pray," Nell said indignantly. "I am presenting myself for the issuance of a warrant for my imminent arrest."

"Not so fast," said Maya. "We're not so sure we want to issue a warrant for your arrest."

"Yeah. Where's Liza Lotsa?" Ben said. "We want to talk to her."

Nell suddenly looked very cagey. "As her attorney," she said, "I have advised her to resist all attempts at coercion. She is in protective custody at this time."

"Oh, yeah? Whose protective custody?"

"Er, mine," said Nell.

"Well, if you're her attorney," said Maya, "you'd better cough her up. We want to talk to her."

"I'm afraid that will be impossible," said Nell.

"Why?"

"Her whereabouts are unknown to me at this time."

"You don't know where she *is*?" said Ben. "Well, where did you see her last?"

"I have no recollection of this fact."

Ben and Maya both rolled their eyes. "Lawyer talk," muttered Maya.

"You know what I think?" Ben said to Maya. "I think Nell is just here to waste our time and get us to issue another phony warrant while Liza gets away again. Aren't you?" he demanded of Nell.

"I refuse to answer on the grounds that it may incriminate me," said Nell.

"Ben, I think you're right," said Maya. "Nell, where is Liza?"

"No comment," said Nell.

By this time the crowds were all gone and the train had slowly pulled out of the station. They had already been there for about twenty minutes. Maya took a deep breath and counted to ten to keep from bopping Nell. "All right," she said finally. "Let's do it another way. If I told you I thought Liza was at the Great Salt Lake, would you tell me that was wrong?" Maya figured that as Liza's lawyer, Nell couldn't actually lie; it must be against some kind of lawyer rule.

"I would refrain from comment."

Ben and Maya exchanged a look. Nell hadn't told Maya she was wrong, and that must mean Liza was at the lake.

"That's all I need to know," said Maya. "Let's go, Ben."

"Out of the way, Nell," said Ben.

They hustled past her down the platform, following the exit signs, and finally ran out into the street. A line of taxicabs waited outside the station. "Take us to the Great Salt Lake, please," said Maya. "And step on it."

"Yes, ma'am," said the driver.

They took off in a hurry, moving fast through the streets of Salt Lake City. Four blocks from the station they passed a huge stone-walled square. Inside it was a great stone building with six spires. It looked like a cathedral.

"What's that?" Ben asked the cabdriver.

"That's the Mormon Temple," replied the cab-driver. "It took forty years to build. It's the most important building for the Mormons. You can't even go in there if you're not a Mormon."

"The Mormons were the first settlers in Utah, right?" Maya asked the driver.

"That's right. Brigham Young came here in 1847 with a hundred forty-three men and three women, and they decided this was the place to settle down. This whole city sprang up after that."

They kept on going, heading north now. "How far is the Great Salt Lake?" Maya asked.

"Not far at all. You can smell the salt air from here."

Maya took a deep sniff. "It smells like the ocean," she said.

"Only it's about seven times saltier," said the driver. "It's at the bottom of the Great Basin, like a big bowl. Water comes in, but it can't drain out. So it just evaporates, leaving the salt behind. You can float great in it."

In just a little while they were there. It seemed to stretch out forever in front of them, with little waves lapping at the sandy beaches, and seagulls wheeling overhead. In the distance they could see big piles of salt and minerals that were being extracted from the lake to be sold.

"It's huge!" Maya exclaimed.

"Our biggest lake west of the Great Lakes," said the cabdriver. "Largest salt lake in the western hemisphere. That'll be fourteen dollars, please."

They paid the cabdriver, thanked him for the tour, and got out. The cab drove off.

"Now what?" asked Ben as the seagulls cried above them.

"I don't know," said Maya, "but these were just about the right coordinates on the map. Let's see what happens."

11
Salt Lake City, Utah

Ben and Maya shaded their eyes as they looked out over the sparkling lake. There were lots of boats, big and small, skimming over the salty water.

Nearby there was a small marina, with boats tied up to the docks. Ben and Maya walked down the road to take a look.

There were all sorts of pleasure boats there—sailboats, yachts, and dinghies. There was also one larger yacht, with the sleek lines of a racing boat. As they got closer, they could see the name of the boat painted on the hull: *Lotsa Trouble*.

"Omigosh! It's her!" Maya gasped.

As if on cue, the yacht's powerful motor started

up. A sleek arm snaked out from the cabin and untied the rope that moored the boat to the dock.

"She's going to get away!" cried Ben. "What should we do?"

Maya looked around wildly. "There!" she said. "There's a man in a boat. Maybe he can help us."

They ran over to the man, who was fussing with the motor on a blue-and-white powerboat. "Sir!" called Maya. "Can you help us? We need to follow that yacht!"

He laughed. He had a deep suntan and white, white hair, and he looked nice. "That's the first time I've heard that one," he said. "Follow that yacht, eh? Well, why not? Get in and we'll see what we can do. My name's Will, by the way."

Ben and Maya introduced themselves, and they hurriedly shook hands.

Will pulled the rope to start the motor, and it roared to life. It sounded reassuringly loud.

"Do you think we could catch her in this?" Ben asked.

"Oh, it's a her?" said Will. "Then I certainly hope we can catch her. Is she pretty?"

"You wouldn't want to catch this one, believe me," said Maya. "She's bad, bad news."

"Story of my life," Will said, grinning. He gunned the motor.

The yacht was a few hundred yards ahead of them and seemed to be the faster of the two boats. The distance widened between them every minute.

"Rats!" said Maya. "We're going to lose her."

At that moment the yacht slowed down, and then it stopped. What was going on?

A shadow passed over them, and the already loud noise of the speedboat's motor was drowned out by a much louder *whump-whump-whump* sound. They looked up to see a helicopter directly overhead—heading for the yacht.

"Son of a gun!" said Will, his hair whipping around his head from the helicopter's wind. He kept steering for the yacht.

When the helicopter was directly over the yacht, it hovered there, and a rope ladder descended from its belly. In a moment the lovely Liza Lotsa was scrambling up the ladder. She carried a large canvas bag.

"Rats, rats, rats!" Maya repeated.

Liza disappeared into the helicopter, and the

ladder was hauled up. The copter headed north across the lake.

"So close!" groaned Ben. "We were so close, and we've lost her again!"

"And she *was* pretty," said Will.

Ben and Maya sat in the speedboat with their heads in their hands.

"So," said Will, "what now?"

Ben looked at the yacht. "I guess maybe we ought to board the yacht and see if we can find anything that will tell us where she's going," he said.

"Can I ask, now that we have a little time, exactly what's going on here?" said Will.

"We're ACME agents," explained Ben, "and that woman is a wanted criminal. We think she's stolen the colors from the Painted Desert." Ben pulled out his ACME badge to show Will.

"What is that, a toy?" asked Will.

Ben just sighed.

Will gunned the speedboat and they headed for the yacht. He pulled up alongside it and cut the motor.

"Be careful," Ben whispered to Maya as she began clambering up onto the larger boat. "There could still be somebody in there."

"You don't need to whisper," said Maya. "It's not like they couldn't hear us coming. Besides," she added, "you don't seriously think there's anybody left on this boat, do you? Liza Lotsa is long gone. She's just leading us around the country on a wild-goose chase. It's her idea of fun. Or maybe Carmen's idea. Are you coming or not?" She threw her right leg over the railing of the yacht and flopped into the boat.

"Okay, okay," said Ben.

Less easily, he pulled himself up onto the larger boat, and Maya yanked him aboard.

It was a beautiful boat, all varnished mahogany and polished brass. "Well," said Maya, looking around, "if there's one thing we know Liza Lotsa has, it's style."

"Not much here to help us, though," said Ben, lifting the foam cushions on the seats. "She didn't leave a thing to tell us where she's going next."

"Hold on, maybe she did," Maya called from the stairs that led belowdecks. "Come look at this, Ben!"

"Be there in a second," Ben called back. He was interested in the instrument panel.

"I think you better come *now*," Maya shouted.

113

Ben flew down the narrow, steep stairs, afraid Maya had encountered something dangerous. But what she was staring at was the flickering screen of a computer.

"There's stuff on the screen," Maya said, "but it's all disappearing. It's as if it's being eaten up or something."

Ben quickly slid into the seat that was bolted to the floor in front of the computer, which was also bolted down. On the screen, the words and letters were disintegrating before his eyes, breaking up into tiny bits and then going *poof.*

"Rats," he said. "I think she programmed a virus into it so the information would destroy itself before we got here." He began hurriedly tapping keys. "Maybe I can save it," he said.

Maya hung anxiously over his shoulder and watched.

AUTO—SELF-DESTRUCT PROGRAM IN PROGRESS, said the message on the screen.

Ben tried something else. ACCESS DENIED.

"Rats, rats, rats!" he yelled.

AUTO-DESTRUCT WILL BE COMPLETE IN 20 SEC-ONDS, said the screen. Then the numbers started ticking down: 19, 18, 17 . . .

"One last thing to try," said Ben, his fingers flying on the keyboard.

AUTO-DESTRUCT PROGRAM TERMINATED, it said. HAVE A NICE DAY. The countdown was stopped at four seconds.

"Whew!" said Ben and Maya gustily.

"Now, let me see what's left," said Ben. "There may be nothing usable."

He worked on the computer, taking his time now. Screen after screen came up, the letters too destroyed to read.

"Maybe it was working its way to the end," said Ben. He scrolled the screens down to the end of the file.

Most of the last screen was too broken up to read, but it got progressively better at the bottom. With some effort, it was possible to make out the last two lines:

CARMEN

BETWEEN CRIPPLE AND SAFETY, it said.

Ben put his chin in his hand. "Cripple and safety," he mused. "Is Carmen going to do something bad to a crippled person—like, before they reach safety?"

"That's doesn't sound like Carmen," said Maya.

"She would never actually hurt someone. And she'd never let her operatives do it either."

"I know, I know," said Ben. "I'm just thinking here."

Maya paced up and down the tiny room, which served as a combination bedroom, kitchen, and living room. "Cripple and safety," she repeated. "Cripple and safety. What are we supposed to do with that?" She paced some more. "We can't have come so far, just to hit a wall now. I won't let that happen."

Ben, meanwhile, was squinting at the computer screen. "You know," he said, "I can almost make out a word here near the bottom."

Maya leaped to his side. "Where?"

Ben pointed to a word on the screen. It had four letters.

"It starts with an *N*," said Maya.

"Definitely. And it ends with an *E*."

"Look at that third letter," said Maya. "Could it be an *N*?"

"I don't think so. Look, you can just make out two points at the top. I think it's an *M*, Maya."

"Okay. So it's *N*, blank, *M*, *E*," said Maya.

"Name?" suggested Ben.

"It doesn't look like an *A*," said Maya, peering at the screen. "I think it has a little curve to it. I can see a tiny bit of a curve."

"I think you're right. So it's not an *A* or an *I*."

"Or an *E*. That leaves a *U* or an *O*."

"Nume. Or Nome. Isn't a nome one of those little weird guys, like a troll?" asked Ben.

"No, Mr. Geography Genius-Not. You're thinking of a *g*nome, with a *g*. Nome's a place. It's in Alaska. Maybe that's where she went."

"Great!" said Ben, too excited to be insulted. "It's something, anyhow. Let's call Yul. The worst that can happen is we'll go there and we won't find anything. We don't lose anything by it."

"Okay. But let's make sure Nume isn't a place too."

Ben dialed Yul on the Sender.

"Ah, my little chickadees," said the ever-cheerful Yul. "How goes the hunt?"

"It's going," said Ben. "Maybe. We think we need to go to Nome. Unless there's a place called Nume."

"Let me check," said Yul. "Nope," he said. "Can't turn up anyplace in the U.S. called Nume. I guess you're going to Nome. Got some warm clothes? It's way far north."

"We actually do," said Ben, suddenly thinking fondly of his parka and mittens in the plastic bag.

"Listen, Yul," said Maya, "would you happen to know about any kind of facility in Nome for people who can't walk? Like a big hospital or rehabilitation center?"

"Can't say I know Nome that intimately. Tell me why you're asking, though, and maybe I can help you."

Maya told him about *cripple* and *safety*, and Yul twisted his mouth to one side, thinking. "Those words ring a faint little bell," he said. "Let me ponder."

He pondered.

"Hah!" he said, smacking his forehead. "They're not just words. They're *places*. Checkpoints, to be exact. Along the Iditarod trail."

"What's that?"

"The Iditarod is a gigantic dogsled race through Alaska. It's over a thousand miles, goes over mountains, coastlines, frozen rivers, you name it. They call it the Last Great Race on Earth. And," he said, flipping through one of the thousands of books he had at Travel Central, "it's going on *right now*!"

"Holy moley," said Ben. "So Liza is meeting Carmen along the trail of the Iditarod."

"Between Cripple and Safety!" said Maya.

"Now," said Yul, "we'll have to figure out how to get you there. Let's see. I can put you in a regular plane to Anchorage—that's where the race starts. Then you'll meet up with Yukon Connie, one of our agents up north. I believe she has a small propeller plane. She should be able to fly you into Cripple."

"Thanks, Yul," said Ben. "You've been great. I hope you don't have to do this too many more times."

"As many times as it takes," said Yul. "Just so you catch the bad guys."

Ben said good-bye to Yul, and he and Maya climbed the stairs. Their friend in the speedboat was still there, waiting for them.

"Back to shore?" he asked.

"Back to shore, please, Will," said Maya. "We're going to the Iditarod!"

12
Anchorage, Alaska

The flight to Anchorage was a bumpy one, and Ben and Maya began feeling a little green very soon. Ben decided to call The Chief and let her know what was going on. Maybe it would keep his mind off his stomach.

"I just hope you're right this time," said The Chief. "Another wrong warrant would be a real black eye for ACME."

"I hope we're right, too," said Ben.

"We're about to pack it in and come back to Headquarters," said The Chief. "I think this date line thing was some kind of sick joke from Carmen. In fact, I'm beginning to think she's figured out how to tap into the CrimeNet. We've changed all the codes, just in case. She won't do that again, that's for sure."

When Ben and Maya staggered off the plane, Yukon Connie was waiting for them. She was a tiny young woman, no taller than Maya.

"No time to lose," she said. "The mushers are already starting to check in at Cripple."

"What's a musher?" Ben asked.

"Mushers are dogsled drivers," she explained. "It comes from the French word *marcher*, which means 'to walk.' Like in 'Forward, march!'"

"Which is what we'd better do if we're going to catch up to Liza," said Maya.

"Yup," agreed Connie. "Let's hop into my Cessna and hightail it up there."

There was nothing Ben and Maya wanted to do less than get back onto a plane, especially a small one, but there was no other choice. The wind howled as they hustled across the airfield to Connie's plane, and the kids pulled their fur-trimmed parka hoods tightly around their faces.

"It's a little tight in here," said Connie, folding her compact body into the cockpit. "Just make yourselves as comfortable as you can."

In a few minutes they had climbed into the sky and were flying over the frozen mountains north of Anchorage. The plane went up and down, and Ben's and Maya's stomachs went with it.

"Know anything about the Iditarod?" Connie shouted over the roar of the engine.

"Not much," Maya shouted back.

"Well, the first Iditarod run wasn't a race at all. It was a mercy mission. Back in 1925, a lot of folks in Nome were getting diphtheria. In those days people used to die during diphtheria epidemics. It was a dread disease. Now, at that time there was no way to get the diphtheria medicine all the way up there except by dogsled. So about twenty mushers and their huskies formed a kind of relay team, handing the antitoxin off to a fresh team at every checkpoint. They saved a lot of lives. The race commemorates that story."

"Cool," shouted Maya.

"How long does the race take?" Ben asked.

"About two, three weeks," said Connie.

There was little talking after that, as Ben and Maya concentrated on holding down the lunches they'd had on their first plane ride.

After about an hour, the plane started flying

into light snow. By the time another ten minutes had passed, the snow was heavy, and then blinding. Ben and Maya clutched the edges of their seats tensely.

"I was hoping we'd miss this," said Connie. "It's bad news for you, unfortunately. I'm going to have to make an instrument landing in Takotna. That's just two checkpoints before Cripple."

"And then what'll we do?" Maya wailed.

"Plan B." Connie grinned. "You're going to learn how to mush, and quick. I'm going to radio ahead and have Klondike Ike meet you at Takotna with teams and supplies. He's the other ACME agent in Alaska, and he knows all about huskies. He'll help you get where you're going."

Klondike Ike was a huge fellow with a big black beard and wild hair. He had come to meet them with two sleds and two teams, each consisting of ten dogs harnessed together. The dogs all had little booties on their feet. "Welcome to the great frozen North!" he said heartily. "You're about to have the ride of your lives."

"But we don't know how to mush!" said Ben.

"Tell you what I'm going to do," said Ike. "I'm

going to handle the first sled and lead the way. I'll take one of you. The other one will take the second sled. Who's the most athletic?"

Ben pointed to Maya.

"I guess that would be me," she agreed. "Why do I have to be athletic?"

"Because sometimes you'll fall off the sled and have to catch up, and sometimes you'll have to run alongside the sled to give the dogs a break."

"Oh, wow," said Maya. "What am I getting into?"

"It'll be fine. I'll be right beside you. All you have to remember is that when you deal with a team of sled dogs, you're the boss. They'll get all confused if they don't know that for sure."

"How do I tell them?"

"For one thing, you need to know the commands. To get them moving, you say 'Hike!' Turn left is 'Haw,' and right is 'Gee.' And when you want to slow down, you say, 'Easy.' Got it?"

"Got it. I think."

"Your lead dog's name is Spike. He's a sweetheart."

Maya scratched Spike behind the ears for a minute, and then they shoved off.

"Hike!" said Ike.

"Hike!" said Maya, trying to sound as much like the boss as possible. To her great relief, it seemed to work.

Very soon they were gliding over the snow at a great clip. Fir trees whizzed past them on both sides. Ben got to sit on the sled, bundled up in a blanket, but Ike and Maya stood.

"I didn't bring very big teams, because we're only doing a little section of the trail. Just until we catch up with Liza and Carmen." Ike shouted over his shoulder so Maya could hear him.

"How do you keep from getting lost?" Maya called to him.

"See those marks painted on the trees? Those are called blazes. They mark the trail."

After a little while Ike pulled a cellular phone out of the pocket of his parka. "Just a little touch of the ACME agent along the trail," he said. "I'm going to call ahead to the checkpoint at Cripple and find out if Carmen or Liza Lotsa checked in there yet." He made a short call, and then put the phone away. "Not there yet," he said. "We're not pulling much gear, so we should be able to gain on them. Maybe we'll catch up with them soon."

"My question," said Ben, "is why on earth are they here? What are they *doing* here?"

"We'll find out, I'm sure. Maybe they're enjoying the race," said Maya, "but there's some other reason, something that has to do with the Painted Desert. I'd bet a lot on it."

"Holy cow!" said Ben suddenly. "I just remembered something. We never got a warrant for Liza. When we catch up with her, we won't be able to arrest her."

"Guess you'd better get on the Sender to Wanda again," said Maya. "I just hope we're right this time."

"We're right. You know we are." Ben pulled the Sender out of his pocket and punched in the code for Wanda the Warrant Officer.

"Wanda here," said Wanda, coming in on the video screen.

"Wanda," said Ben, "we need a warrant for the arrest of Liza Lotsa. And in a hurry, too. Can you do it?"

"Can I do it?" snorted Wanda. "What do you think I do around here all day, anyhow?"

"Sorry, Wanda."

"It'll be through to you in about half an hour."

"Can you possibly make it any faster?"

"For you, anything."

"Thanks, Wanda."

They kept dashing along the trail, and now they were occasionally passing a team. Ike would wave at them as they passed. "Just out for a spin," he'd call. "Don't worry."

Ben and Maya scrutinized every musher, looking for Liza. No luck yet.

"Hey, kids," said Ike. "You're in for a real northern treat. Look up in the sky."

Ben and Maya looked up, and gasped in wonder. Above them, high over the treetops in the just-darkening sky, there was an incredible, shimmering curtain of colored light—oranges, reds, chocolates, lavenders, greens, purples. It was the most amazing thing either of them had ever seen.

"Those are the northern lights," said Ike. "The aurora borealis." He looked up at it, smiling, happy to be sharing it with newcomers.

"What *is* it?" Maya asked.

"Well, it's pretty hard to explain," said Ike. "You know the North Pole's kind of like a big huge magnet, right?"

"Right," said Maya. "That's why the compass always points there."

"Okay. Well, that magnet also attracts energy from the sun. And when the energy hits the earth's atmosphere, we see the aurora. Beautiful, isn't it?"

They watched the rippling light together, their eyes wide with wonder.

But then his face changed. His smile disappeared. He looked puzzled. He looked disturbed.

"What's the matter?" Ben asked him.

"It's the colors. They're strange. Something's happened to them, I just don't know what. They're supposed to be red, yellow, green, blue, and violet."

Maya looked hard at the aurora, and then something clicked into place in her brain. "I know what," she said.

"Oh, jeepers!" said Ben. "I know what, too!"

"Could you clue me in, please?" said Ike.

"It's the colors from the Painted Desert! She's hidden them in the aurora borealis!" said Ben.

"And there she is!" said Maya, pointing down the trail. "Look!"

A flash of bright red was disappearing around a curve up ahead.

"Carmen!" said Ike. "I've never actually gotten to see her! And there she is, big as life!"

He urged the dogs on, and they sped up.

"There!" cried Ben. "Beyond that clearing!"

"And there's Liza with her," said Maya. "In the same brown parka she was wearing in St. Paul, remember, Ben?"

"How could I forget?"

They could see the two figures more closely now. They were both bent down beside one of the sleds, fussing with the supplies lashed to it.

"They must have met up ahead of schedule because they knew we were on their trail," said Maya.

"If we do this right," said Ben, "we can catch them both. Wouldn't that be incredible?"

"Then we'd be out of the doghouse, permanently!" said Maya. "Ike, can we slow down and sneak up on them?"

"Sure," said Ike. He called softly to his dogs. "Easy," he said.

"Easy," said Maya to her team. The dogs slowed down.

"Ike," Maya said as quietly as she could, "maybe you can sneak around to the right, and I'll go left. We'll get them between us so they can't get away."

"Good idea," said Ike. He clicked to his dogs and said, "Gee."

And then, without warning, all heck broke loose. A tremendous wind threatened to blow them off the trail, and there was a deafening noise from the sky. The dogs began to howl in alarm.

Maya, Ben, and Ike looked up in confusion, and at that moment over the next ridge came three enormous helicopters. They were painted in green-and-brown camouflage, and they had powerful lights that swept the ground, searching the whole area.

"What on earth—?" said Ike.

A loud siren began to blare from one of the helicopters, and then it stopped. They all heard a microphone click on.

"Carmen Sandiego and Liza Lotsa," said a woman's voice. *"You are under arrest for the theft of the colors from the Painted Desert. Do not attempt to escape."*

The Chief!

Maya and Ben could hardly believe their ears. What was she doing here?

The three helicopters began lowering themselves to the ground, and as they got closer, they created havoc below them. Their tremendous, powerful rotors churned the air, whipping up the snow into a blinding white-out.

"Oh, no!" wailed Maya. "We can't see them! They're going to get away! Our beautiful plan to sneak up on them is ruined!"

The helicopters touched down, but it took a few minutes for the chaos to subside. With the rotors still turning slowly, The Chief stepped down from one of the choppers, brandishing a warrant. She looked around until she saw what she was looking for: the figure in the bright-red coat and fedora, diving behind a boulder.

"You can't get away from us this time!" said The Chief. Then she spotted the kids, who were making their way over to her on snowshoes.

"Great work, kids," she said. "We realized you were right all along. There was nothing going on at the date line. We found proof that Carmen had cracked the CrimeNet codes. So we came up here to give you ACME support, help you make the collar."

"But—" said Ben.

One of the other ACME agents had lunged behind the boulder and was now dragging out the figure in red.

"Aha!" crowed The Chief. "At last—we've got you this time, Carmen."

The agent whipped the fedora off the figure's head, to reveal—curly black hair?

It was Liza Lotsa.

Liza doubled over laughing. "You silly people!" she giggled. "You and your helicopters made such a big mess, it was easy for me to switch coats with Carmen. You'll never get her—never! Ha ha ha ha!" She was still laughing as the agent clapped the handcuffs on her.

"Look!" cried Maya. "Up there!"

A figure in a brown parka was streaking over a hill in the distance, much too far away to catch up with.

Ben and Maya were in agony. "We almost had her!" said Ben. His fists were clenched helplessly. "If only those helicopters hadn't . . ."

"Let it go, Ben," said Maya. She blinked away one little tear, took a deep breath, and turned away. "We'll get her next time. Sometimes stuff just happens."

As they watched, the figure turned for a moment, waved at them, and disappeared.

"Rats!" said The Chief.

*   *   *

133

Well, that was lots of fun. Those kids are better than even I realized. They came just a little too close for comfort. When The Chief realizes what good detectives they are, she'll give them a promotion to Detective First Class for sure. Then they'll be even more fun to match wits against. Any two detectives who'll run up the Empire State Building and mush across Alaska to get me are worthy opponents indeed.

Of course, this game's over now. Tomorrow I'll make a bargain, trade Liza's freedom for the safe return of the Painted Desert's colors. Everything will be the way it was, even the Painted Desert grubby snake, or whatever it's called. Everyone will be happy. And then it will be time to start planning my next little caper. . . .

Carmen Sandiego™ Challenges Kids to Discover the World!

Look for the "Official Carmen Sandiego Clue Book," available at bookstores and software retailers nationwide.

Ages 9 & up
USA Geography
and Regional Cultures
WIN/MAC CD-ROM

Ages 9 & up
World Geography and Cultures
WIN/MAC CD-ROM

- -

Save $20

Purchase New Editions of both "Where in the World is Carmen Sandiego?" AND "Where in the USA is Carmen Sandiego?" CD-ROM geography games, and get $20 back.*

To receive $20 rebate by mail:

1. Complete this **original** rebate coupon (no photocopies, please);
2. Include the **original** sales receipt(s) indicating your qualifying purchases of **each** New Edition;
3. Complete product registration cards for **both** products.

4. **Mail all items to:**
Carmen Mystery Book Offer
P.O. Box 52929, Dept. 2625
Phoenix, AZ 85072-2929

Name _____ Address _____

City _____ State _____ Zip _____ Daytime Phone ( ) _____

Brøderbund